THE MAN WITH THE RUBBER FACE

H. BEDFORD-JONES

THE MAN
WITH THE
RUBBER FACE

H. BEDFORD-JONES

ILLUSTRATIONS BY
FRANK BENSING

STEEGER BOOKS • 2025

TABLE OF CONTENTS

THE MAN WITH THE RUBBER FACE

THE MAN WITH THE RUBBER FACE

FOLLOW THE ASTOUNDING ADVENTURES OF JOHN CABOT, WHO
COULD CHANGE HIS IDENTITY AT WILL, AND WHO USED HIS
UNCANNY POWERS IN A PRIVATE WAR ON THE UNDERWORLD

JOHN CABOT caught up the speaking tube, as the black limousine sped into the city. The heavy-jawed, bull-necked chauffeur was one of two men in the world whom he could trust.

"Bowker! Stop at the next corner. By that police box. Don't open the door."

The limousine swung in to the curb. Cabot's gaze stabbed up and down the street, making sure no officer was in sight. Opening the car door, he swung out to the sidewalk, took a key from his pocket, then unlocked the police box. As he took down the receiver, he directed a cheerful smile at the startled Bowker.

"Hello, sergeant! Get this," he said rapidly. "The Carson child snatching was pulled off by Lefty Flynn and his moll. The child is with Flynn's grandmother, same name, back room of tenement at 783 Blucher Street. Safe and unhurt. Get her quick, and grab Flynn."

He closed the box and darted into the limousine. It roared away instantly.

Ten minutes later, Cabot was sitting in the private office of his lawyer, whose windows looked out over the city's skyline. He was laughing, healthily bronzed, a certain reckless devil-may care look of youth and high spirits in his features.

"John, why the devil did you do it?" demanded the older man earnestly. "You, to play the part of a cheap trickster, a penny magician—"

"Hold everything! By the Lord, I was good at it; and today

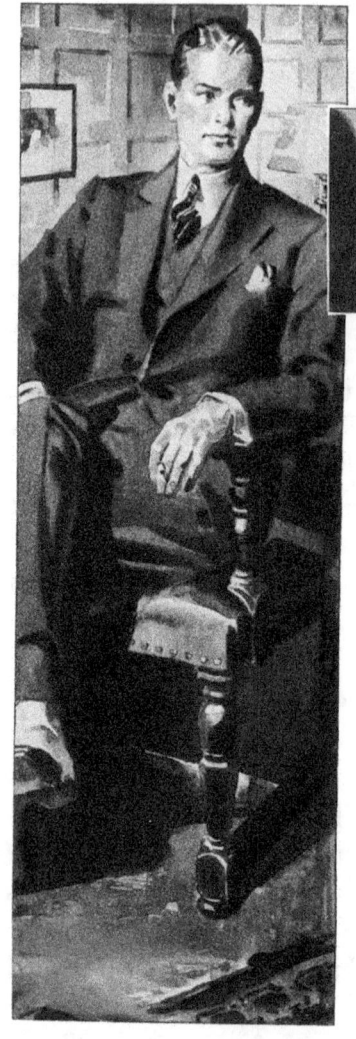

"I don't intend to escape the past," said John Cabot defiantly, "I intend to master it."

I'm better," cut in Cabot gaily. "Why? To earn a living of course. I took the name of Larry Kilraine; my professional monicker was Korvo the Great. And that means something!"

"So does the penitentiary, John."

"Under the name of Kilraine, remember," said Cabot with a cool smile. "And I'm pardoned. Eighteen months served, of a ten-year stretch."

*The man who got
out of the car was
Larry Kilraine.*

Thanks to a prison break, and the luck that served you in helping—"

"Luck? No! Brains!" said Cabot. "And only you and Bowker know that John Cabot has been in the big house. I get out to find that my uncle is dead and you're holding the Cabot estate for me. Call that luck, if you like!"

The lawyer eyed him keenly. "You're supposed to have been

traveling in Africa. Have you given up your bitterness against Morse?"

CABOT'S FACE darkened. "That rat? Morse, a mere bank clerk, has now become Morse the broker. He got a ten-thousand dollar start; he sent Kilraine to jail for the theft. A man he scarcely knew! He's a big shot now, and a crook. No! The prime object of my young life is to put that bird where he belongs. By the way, what about a secretary for me?"

"She's waiting outside. But I'm doubtful about you."

Cabot smiled sunnily. "How? Oh! Let me use that telephone a minute, will you?"

He took up the desk phone and called a number. The sunlight struck on his hair, turned its grayish brown to gold. Gray hair and a young face—

"This you, Viola?" he said abruptly. A sharp change leaped into his voice; it was suddenly harsh, throaty, deep "Larry Kilraine—sure thing! Nevermind. Have you kept my offices as I wrote you? Good girl. Meet me there in an hour."

He hung up, leaned back, met the intent gaze of the lawyer.

"That's exactly it, John," said the latter gravely. "You've a past. You can't escape it. That's why I'm doubtful about you."

Cabot laughed. "I don't intend to escape it; I intend to master it! If I was a magician two years ago, now I'm a wizard! I've learned things, I tell you; learned things! I'm going to put some of these men who are a living menace to humanity, where they belong. You've heard of the Carson kidnaping case?"

"Who hasn't?" asked the lawyer, frowning. "A mystery—"

"Bah! Korvo the Great snaps his fingers at mystery!" said Cabot. "Within an hour there'll be extras on the street telling of the child's recovery and the capture of her snatchers. Who brought it about? I did. You understand? Not a soul knows but I did it! I looked into the rotten heart of an underworld rat and—"

The sudden flame that sprang in his face died away. As though afraid of letting himself go, he checked his words, leaned back, shrugged.

"Well, never mind. Come; what about the secretary? I need one at once. The estate is getting balled up. I had to fire that fool who was running it, you see."

THE LAWYER sighed. "John. I don't understand you. If what you say is true, you've done a big thing but let it pass. This girl is one whom you knew as a child; she's forced to earn a living now. She can handle your affairs capably and honestly. Mary Sargent."

"What? Why, she lived near us! I remember her; a long-legged little tyke with two braids, sure! I used to fight with her."

Breaking into a laugh, the lawyer pressed a button. A moment later John Cabot came to his feet, incredulous. This trim, smiling girl with softly waved golden hair, with level, unafraid eyes—

"Mary Sargent, by all that's holy! Are you my new secretary?"

"That depends," she replied, laughing. "Do you remember the horrid little boy who so violently shoved me out on a freshly tarred street one day?"

"And spoiled your new shoes? Yes." Cabot turned to the lawyer. "You're ruled out, old man. This applicant is going for a walk with her new boss. Too much legal atmosphere around here to talk business as it should be talked! Come on, Mary! I'll walk home with you. Still live in the old house?"

She did.

Presently, Bowker had his instructions, and John Cabot was swinging along beside the girl, both of them talking rapidly. He was amazed by her quick vivacity, by the impulsive life-joy springing within her. Despite poverty and struggles, despite grief and hardship, she seemed to meet all that swam into her ken with an upsurging zest, a straightforward eagerness, looking life straight in the eye and liking it.

"God, what a girl!" thought Cabot.

When they parted, it was arranged. Mary Sargent was in

*At nine in the morning, Mary Sargent was
in full possession of Cabot's office.*

charge of the Cabot estate, was given an office key, and was left
to take things over the same afternoon.

Cabot came to where the black limousine awaited him. He
stepped in, pulled down the window blinds, and gave Bowker
an address. Bowker, whom he had known in jail, whom he had
found a man of steel, whom he had pulled from the mire of
gangster life—a man to trust, was Bowker!

And now John Cabot fell hurriedly to work. Panels opened in
unsuspected places, a drawer popped out, a mirror sprang into
sight. From a grip at his feet, he took clothes, shabby but neat.
Korvo the Great was invariably neat.

WHEN THE limousine halted, it was Larry Kilraine who
alighted.

"It's me that owes you everything, Larry," Viola
said. "I didn't know there were men like you."

He was much taller than John Cabot, hollow-chested. His hooked nose, thin nostrils, black brows, gave him a vulpine appearance. His grayish features were strained, drawn, almost haggard. He stooped at the shoulders, and walked with an odd hesitant swing.

Mounting the steps of a dingy apartment building, he paused at the door and looked up. There at the corner window depended a weather-beaten, half-effaced sign that read:

KORVO THE GREAT
Readings

His lips curling as though in a scornful snarl, he entered the building.

Kilraine unlocked the door of a corner apartment, stepped in, looked around. The place was precisely as he had left it nearly two years ago; but uncleaned, dusty, moldy. A large central reception room. Off to the right was a bedroom, to the left was a small kitchen, both heavily curtained. On the table in the corner window stood a large crystal ball. Black drapes touched with faded scarlet covered the walls. He turned, hearing quick footsteps in the hall.

The half-open door was flung wide. On the threshold appeared a young woman, handsomely dressed. Her dark, exotic loveliness was striking. Her lips were parted, breathless; her alert gaze was fastened upon him in delight, in stirred emotion, in almost incredulous eagerness.

"Larry! I can't believe it—you, you!" Kilraine extended his hand, and smiled in casual greeting.

"Hello, Viola. Good of you to keep the old office just as it was. How are you?"

She closed the door, suddenly caught his arm. "Larry! It—it wasn't a break?"

"Lord, no! I'm pardoned," said Kilraine.

He produced a packet of cheap cigarettes and lit one, after she had refused.

"A prison revolt; an ugly murderous mess. I was of service, and drew a pardon. Let it pass. I don't want to discuss it."

"When was all this?" she demanded, her great dark eyes riveted on his face.

"Six weeks ago."

She started. "And you never let me know! You never wrote me! Oh, Larry!"

Kilraine made a gesture of irritation, or distaste. He pulled up a chair and almost forced her into it, then watched her steadily.

"LET'S HAVE an understanding, Viola. We worked together three years. I picked you up, gave you a new life, made you my assistant, helped you to become the sort of woman you'd dreamed about. Do I owe you explanations?"

The reproachful, hurt look died from her face. Her head drooped a little.

"No, Larry; it's me that owes you everything!" she said in a low voice. "I've been living for the time when I could make it up to you. Why, I didn't know there were men as white as you, Larry Kilraine! You've never asked for a thing. You know there's nothing you couldn't have for the asking, and yet—"

"Never mind all that," he intervened curtly. "I was suddenly jerked off on a ten-year stretch, framed on a charge of theft by that damned rat, Morse. I saw that you were kept in funds, asked you to remain on the level. Have you done it?"

A slight pallor crept into her face as she met his eyes.

"So you're singing in a cabaret," he added. "May I ask why?"

She started. "Who told you?"

"You did. Just now. Neither you nor anyone else can keep anything from me—"

"Oh!" A gasp escaped her.

Then, with a desperate effort, she straightened up.

"I've kept straight, Larry," she said steadily, earnestly. "I've been working for you, for us both. In the old days we were cheap pikers. Now, I've got things lined up to put us on ice for life; big stuff! You can do it. I got that cabaret job, not for the money, but to meet men of all kinds. I've done it. I've found out about Morse, for one thing. He's a broker, but he's in other things, too. I've got his chief helper on the string. Morse has done a lot of blackmailing, understand?"

Kilraine nodded. "Then I can count on you?"

"For anything, Larry. You know that! Anything and everything!"

"Good." Kilraine glanced at his watch. "Meet me tonight at the little Greek café. Say, six-thirty, for dinner. Now, in a few minutes, a man named Flinders will come here, asking for me. I want you to meet him.

She nodded, watching him with intently eager gaze.

"Tell him I'm not here. Size him up. Tell me tonight whether you think he's a mobsman or a dick. I'm going to slip out the other entrance now. Tonight at six-thirty. O.K.?"

"You bet, Larry!"

With a nod, Kilraine stepped into the bedroom. Behind the heavy curtains he drew the sliding doors and locked them. He opened a closet, drew out drawers, and fell to work.

He stripped off his garments, thrust them into a small bag, seated himself before a mirror. The grayish pallor was wiped from his face. Ten years dropped from him. The muscles held in such perfect control, such incredible mastery, relaxed. For an instant he became himself, John Cabot, but only for an instant.

"Now for the test!" he murmured. "If it works on her—then it's infallible!"

AT SIX-THIRTY that evening, Viola entered a small neighboring café, which they had frequented in other days, and found Larry Kilraine seated at a table. She seated herself, took the proferred cigarette, and eyed him with a smile.

"Well, Flinders showed up. Plainclothes dick. Larry, is he after you?"

Kilraine smiled faintly. "No. You'll probably meet him again, later. But I'm curious to hear about Morse. All you know about him."

"It's plenty. But, Larry, hadn't you better let him wait?" Her gaze was pleading, even anxious. "I've got some money saved up, and you must be broke. Hadn't we better go after one of the jobs I've got lined up, and get a stake?"

Kilraine studied her for a moment. "Later, perhaps; not now. First, I'm going after Morse. Except for information, I don't want your help. I'm going to get him, lone-handed."

An hour later they entered the somewhat flashy apartment

building where Viola Le May made her home. Inside Kilraine halted and extended his hand.

"Well, goodnight—"

"Miss Le May!" It was the voice of the telephone girl at the desk. "A gent went up to your room. Said he'd wait for you, and had a key. A real swell-looking gent."

"Thank you," she answered, then turned. She read the look in Kilraine's eyes, and caught at his arm. A storm of passionate entreaty rose in her face.

"Wait, wait! Not what you think, Larry. This is the man I told you about. Ben Carias is his name—"

"Carias—good Lord! Carias, the killer? The East Side gunman?"

"Yes," she breathed. "Morse's man, see? That's why I've played up to him. I can string him along. I've learned a lot—"

"End it. At once!" Kilraine took her hand. "Goodnight. You've got the telephone number safe? Keep it dark. Ask for Cabot, and he'll get me. And remember; end this thing tonight!"

"I will, Larry," she said simply, confidentially.

AT NINE the following morning, Mary Sargeant was in full possession of the headquarters of the Cabot Estate in a downtown building.

She presided over the large outer office, with two stenographers. The inner office was sacred to John Cabot, its own private door opening on the corridor of the building.

Not a block distant, but in a less pretentious building, were the offices of Morse & Company, brokers. Kilraine, calling here about nine-thirty, was informed that Mr. Morse was engaged at the moment. His name was sent in.

"Well, I thought you might be showing up," said Morse challengingly, from behind his flat-topped desk.

He was a plump man, his face unhealthily puffed; but for all that, a wolfish face, small-eyed, vicious, cautious.

"Heard you were out. Got a gun?

"Who, me? Of course not," said Kilraine wonderingly.

"Well, I have. What do you want with me?"

"I've heard a few things about you, Mr. Morse," said Kilraine humbly. "I got tipped off that you might work with me. You know a man named John Cabot? It was in the papers about him a few weeks back."

"Oh! The Cabot estate, sure. I remember it. What's the connection?"

"I've got a letter he wrote" and Kilraine leaned forward. "It shows him up for a thief and a forger, see? He wrote it himself. Never mind where I got it; but if you can work the game so it's safe, I'll split with you. He'll pay big for that letter."

Morse eyed him appraisingly, then held out a plump hand.

"Let's see it."

Kilraine produced a folded paper. Morse spread it out on the desk before him.

"Dear Partner:
   Re our conversation of this a.m. I'll have to make a clean breast of it. I did take your 1st National stock, endorsing it with your name. I had to have the collateral. For God's sake let it ride until I see you.

                              J. CABOT."

Morse whistled softly and leaned back.

"Important if true. A crook, is he? But I'll have to look into it. If this is genuine, we'll hit that bird big; twenty thousand for a starter! Sit down, Kilraine. Have a cigar?"

"No, thanks," replied Kilraine nervously. "Look here! You're not going to gyp me, see? I'm in on this, and I stay in, right to the finish! I aim to be there when he hands over the money, see? I got a photostat of that letter, and—"

"Oh, sure, sure!" Morse reached for a cigar, bit at it, mouthed it. His eyes glittered on Kilraine. "How long would I last if I double-crossed a pal? Forget it. I'll feel out Cabot; if it's O.K., I'll arrange a meeting for tonight. We'll crack him wide open and do it quick. Suit you? Then give me a ring at three this afternoon."

"I guess that's all right," said Kilraine.

Morse gave him a cordial smile.

"What you doing with yourself, anyhow? Need a stake?"

"No, I got enough. Say, you don't think this job will be dangerous?"

"Not the way I handle it!" said Morse expansively. "Nothing to it, absolutely nothing. Well, you give me a ring at three sharp. And all the luck in the world!"

Tho tall, stooping figure of Kilraine departed. The door closed.

"YOU DAMNED rat!" spat Morse viciously.

Naturally unaware of the sentiments animating Morse, Larry Kilraine sought the street and in five minutes was entering the building where the Cabot Estate was housed. He left the elevator at the ninth floor, passed the Cabot offices, and halted at a blind door.

Unlocking this, he entered the private sanctum of John Cabot. As he closed the door, the private-line telephone on the big desk was buzzing. He darted to it swiftly.

"Mr. Cabot speaking—"

"Get Kilraine! For God's sake, get Kilraine, quick!" It was the voice of Viola Le May.

"Oh, sure! Wait a minute." Pausing, Kilraine changed to the throatier, harsher tones that Viola knew so well. "Hello? Who is it?"

"Larry! Get over here, quick—my God, Larry, it's awful! I can't tell you over the wire. You've got to help me, save me—"

"I'll be right over."

Bowker was not on hand. A taxicab took him rapidly across town to the garish apartment building.

When Viola opened the door, he found her calm—dreadfully, horribly calm.

"In the front room, Larry," she said, white as death. Kilraine shoved past her.

He saw Carias' sprawled figure by the mantel.

"You killed him?"

"No! I didn't!" she burst out passionately. "Last night I turned him out. Just now, before I telephoned, he walked in on me. He grabbed me. Said he was going to take me out of here, to his car. I—I fought him. Tripped him. He fell and hit his head—look!"

It was true. There was no blood on the dead man's head, scarcely a bruise. The killer had fallen, hitting his temple against the gas logs. Kilraine swiftly frisked him, handkerchief covering his hand, jerked out the pistol and pocketed it. Then he rose.

"Quiet, now. Keep your head. This is the third floor. Any back entrance?"

"Yes, a kitchen stairs," she answered, starting at him.

"Snap into it, then. Do your act! Get out there, see if it's clear."

She had worked too long with Korvo the Great not to obey him swiftly, in any emergency. Without a word she was gone. Then came her voice.

"All clear, Larry."

"Hold the doors open." Kilraine was following her now, the body of Carias slung over his shoulders. He paused at the rear door, looked her in the eyes. "Get down into the lobby and do it quick. Alibi. Call for a taxicab, go anywhere. I'll get in touch with you tomorrow. Move!"

Then he was gone, down the winding stairs that led to the rear entrance on the alley.

No one on the stairs.

The alley entrance looked clear; a delivery truck stood twenty feet away, motionless. Kilraine paused, peered out, shifted his burden. People were passing, there on the sidewalk. Only one thing to do, only one possible thing!

For the last time, Carias the killer was on his feet, pressed firmly against the wall of the building, in full sight of those who passed. Kilraine held the pistol, handkerchief about the butt to keep off fingerprints. His own were on record—

Bam! Bam-bam! Bam!

The shots roared out, thunderous, reverberating from the walls. The pistol fell to the cement. Ben Carias swayed, his knees were loosened, and he pitched forward on his face. A woman shrieked. Quick shouts pealed up.

Kilraine dodged around the truck and was gone down the alley. Then the unexpected happened. From an entrance darted an officer in uniform, came face to face with him, half turned to follow, then swung back to investigate the uproar.

A moment later Kilraine emerged into another street, wiped sweat from his brow, and fell in with the crowd. It was not yet quite noon. A cold hand seemed to be clamped on the back of his neck. That officer! That one look, shrewd, keen, comprehensive!

"Menace," thought Kilraine. "Danger now, every minute, everywhere! That man will know me again in twenty years from now. Well, that's the gamble."

It was twelve-thirty when Morse was ushered into the private office. He shook hands heartily with John Cabot, accepted a cigarette, and settled into a chair opposite his host.

"I have a rather peculiar errand, Mr. Cabot," he said frankly. "This morning a man came to me with a letter you were supposed to have written. This man is a dangerous character. He's a jailbird, just out of the big house; a dope addict, a scoundrel! He had the insolence to propose that I join him in blackmailing you."

"What!" Cabot lost his smile. "Are you serious?"

"Entirely." Morse extended a typed paper. "Here is a copy of that letter. I believe it to be   "

He did not finish. He was watching Cabot narrowly, and saw how useless were words. For, glancing at the typed lines, Cabot's face changed. He started. A look of keen alarm, of anxiety, flashed into his eyes. Then he glanced up at Morse, and wet his lips.

"This—er—upon my word, Mr. Morse, this is incredible!" he stammered. "How it came into your, hands—"

Morse seized his cue instantly.

"You wrote it, huh? Let's talk business, Cabot," he said with easy familiarity. "You can't afford to have that letter reach the newspapers, then?"

Cabot shrank in his chair. "I—no, no, of course I can't," he said. "A man in my position—it might do me a lot of harm—"

"Nothing to it," said Morse with assurance. "Kilraine wants twenty thousand in cash out of you. I promised to fix it up with you. Now, I propose that this evening he and I will meet you, wherever you say. You'll have the money in marked bills, with detectives waiting to grab him the moment he takes it. The letter will be kept quiet; the police are only too glad to protect people who will persecute these rats. What do you say?"

"In that case, of course, you may count on me," said Cabot nervously. "We might meet at the University Club, say. At seven."

"Fine," and Morse nodded. "But one thing more, Cabot. I'm going to a lot of trouble and risk in this affair. I think you'd better have ten thousand all ready to hand over to me, huh? Before you get the original of the letter."

Cabot stared at him, wet his lips again, blinked.

"I don't understand!" he exclaimed. "Why, that would be blackmail—"

Morse looked him in the eyes, smiling.

"Nonsense! Don't use such a word, Cabot. I'm being of great service to you; saving you from a scoundrel who'd dog you for years, show no mercy! I think you owe me something, don't you?"

"Oh! I suppose—yes, looking at it that way, you're right." And Cabot brightened. "Ten thousand? Of course. I'd cheerfully give that sum, Mr. Morse. Then you'll meet me at the University Club at seven? I'll bring two officers with me."

"And let me tell you something," said Morse. "This Kilraine is a menace to society. We'll put him away for keeps. But don't think that you can doublecross me! Not unless you want that letter made public. It would ruin you."

"I'm afraid it would," said Cabot. "Good heavens, yes!"

"I have a photostat of it, in case you're tempted to double-cross me." And Morse rose. "If you want it given to the papers, just try anything! Otherwise, we're friends."

"My dear fellow, I'm eternally grateful to you!" said Cabot earnestly. "At seven this evening. Come direct to the writing room, will you? We'll be alone there."

AT FIVE minutes to seven that evening, Kilraine and Morse together walked into the University Club.

"Sorry, gentlemen, but Mr. Cabot hasn't been in," said the attendant. "Did you have an appointment?"

"For seven, in the writing room," said Morse. "He asked us to meet him there."

"Then I'll have you taken there at once, and you may wait," was the reply.

In the solemn, silent writing room, quite empty at this hour, Morse seated himself at the central table and motioned his companion to a chair. Kilraine glanced at his hands.

"I'd better brush up a bit, in a place like this," he said.

Morse nodded, scornfully.

"Not a bad idea, Kilraine. You're not even clean. Run along."

"You take care of this, then." Kilraine produced the letter. "I'll be right back."

Morse took the letter, and smiled as the other departed. He lit a cigarette, and his wolfish eyes glittered in anticipation. The clock was just striking seven.

The cigarette was nearly finished when Cabot appeared in the doorway. Morse came to his feet eagerly. Cabot, in evening dress, paused and glanced about.

"All alone, are you?"

"Yes," said Morse. "Kilraine went to the washroom. Back in a minute. All ready?"

Cabot looked at him. "Eh? Oh, certainly! I got the money as you suggested. The bank marked it. Do you want it now?"

"Not me," and Morse smiled. "But we might clean up our little private affair before Kilraine returns. And if you marked my money, God help you!"

"Nonsense, nonsense!" said Cabot, getting out a wallet. He produced ten new, crisp thousand-dollar bills. "There you are, Morse."

The broker nodded and pocketed the notes, then sank back into his chair. Cabot, however, turned and went to the door, and beckoned. Two men, obviously officers in plainclothes, appeared. Cabot pointed to the broker.

"There's your man," he said. "He still has the letter, and the money in marked bills."

Morse leaped to his feet.

"What's this?" he cried out. "Look here! It's Kilraine you want—"

"Kilraine?" returned Cabot icily. "Nonsense. There's no such person. You're the man who visited my office today and demanded ten thousand dollars blackmail!"

Morse stood speechless, as the officers closed in. Then a passionate storm of oaths burst from him.

"You—that rat Kilraine, you double-crossed me!" he shouted. "I'll make this letter public—it'll go to the newspapers—"

"And welcome," said Cabot. "At the first glance at the copy, I knew I'd never written it. It's obviously a forgery. Comparison with my handwriting will undoubtedly prove this. No go, Morse. You and your talk of this unknown Kilraine—"

The handcuffs had clicked. One of the detectives produced the notes and a letter.

"Looks like the evidence, Mr. Cabot."

"You damned double-crosser!" screamed Morse, convulsed with fury. "I'll get you for this—you and that rat Kilraine—"

"He appears subject to delusions officers," said Cabot, regarding the prisoner curiously. "Better get him out of here. I'll be right along."

The two detectives departed with their prisoner.

From his pocket, John Cabot took an evening newspaper and turned to the "scream story" on the front page—the story of how the gangster Ben Carias had that day been put on the spot and riddled with bullets from his own gun. There followed a description of the man who had been seen leaving the scene of the shooting. As a description of Larry Kilraine, it was perfect.

"Too perfect!" murmured Cabot. "Too perfect! That policeman had a camera eye."

And, lighting a cigarette, he followed the officers and their prisoner.

THE MAN WITH THE RUBBER FACE

THE SECOND ASTOUNDING ADVENTURE OF JOHN CABOT—
THE MAN WHO COULD CHANGE HIS IDENTITY AT WILL

A T T H E ninth floor, the elevator opened and Larry Kilraine stepped out. Three men stood by the window at the left; a policeman and two under-cover men, chatting casually.

Kilraine recognized the officer. His pulses leaped. Heart-hurried, he turned right, toward the offices of the Cabot Estate. He was tall, spare, hollow-chested, shabbily but neatly clad. His black brows, thin nostrils and drawn features gave him a haggard, oldish appearance. He walked with a hesitant swing, but rapidly.

The police officer glanced carelessly after him, then stiffened incredulously.

"Glory be! Boys, there's the gun who shot Ben Carias! I saw him leaving there! Come on—we've got him now—"

At the corner of the passage, Kilraine glimpsed their concerted movement. He turned the corner and was gone. Ahead was a blank door into the private office of John Cabot. Nothing else except a washroom and the janitor's closet. He paused at the blank door, slid a key into it, stepped inside. The door closed as the three officers came around the corner. Then it was shaken savagely, vainly.

Two minutes later the policeman and one of his companions, pistols in hand, burst into the outer office. Two stenographers were at work. Mary Sargent, a secretary and manager of the Cabot Estate, was talking with its lawyer, gray-haired Judson

Harmer. Recognizing Harmer as a former police commissioner, the officer saluted hurriedly.

"Morning, sir. Does that blank door on the little corridor enter one of these offices?"

"Yes. Mr. Cabot's private office, said Mary Sargent. "What do you—"

"Show us in there, quick! Which way?"

"Just a minute," intervened Harmer with dignity. "Explain this intrusion, officer!"

"It's the guy who killed Ben Carias, the gunman. I had a glimpse of him after Carias was shot. He went into that office door, sure! Had a key to it!"

"Impossible!" exclaimed Mary Sargent. Harmer, a trifle pale, said nothing. "Unless Mr. Cabot has come in, nobody's there. Look, if you wish; certainly—"

"You stay back, Miss," snapped the officer. "He's cornered, and it means business."

*A scream rang out. Then, red jets, flaming
pistols, roaring shots from every side.
Bullets tore through the parked cars.*

NEXT INSTANT he flung open the door of John Cabot's private office and strode in, followed by his companion. They stopped short. The room was obviously empty—but from the closed toilet cabinet in one corner came a low, cheery whistle. Then the cabinet door was opened. A man in shirt sleeves, drying his hands on a towel, stepped out.

"Hello!" he exclaimed, staring at them in astonishment.

They repaid his stare. John Cabot was not tall nor stooped; his walk was agile, alert. Not a trace of the drawn, fiercely vulpine features that marked Kilraine. His smooth, healthily bronzed face was young.

"Ah, Cabot!" exclaimed the lawyer, pressing forward. "Did anyone come in here?"

Bewildered by their error, finding no possible hiding-place in the room, the two officers departed to join their comrade outside. Harmer closed the door behind them, then turned to the younger man, agitation in his face.

"Good God! Do they really think that you—that Kilraine—murdered Carias?"

"Certainly. I told you what happened." Cabot donned his coat, and dropped into his desk chair. "Sit down and take it easy. They don't know Kilraine by name, fortunately: that officer merely got a glimpse of him, hasn't chanced on the identification yet—"

"This is terrible, terrible!" Harmer strode up and down the room. "I warned you! Once they discover that you're Kilraine, you're ruined! It'll come out that you were in prison, that you earned your living in other days as Korvo the Great, a cheap magician—"

"No! A damned good magician!" Cabot burst into a laugh.

The telephone rang. Cabot answered with his name, heard a woman's voice.

"Please call Mr. Kilraine at once!"

"One minute." Cabot gave the lawyer an amused glance, then leaned forward. His face was changed. As though unconsciously, it narrowed, lengthened, fell into oddly haggard lines. Harmer stared at him, almost in terror. Then Kilraine's harsher, throatier voice sounded.

"Well? Oh, Viola! How are you?"

"Larry! I must see you!" Her voice was athrill with eagerness. "It's one of the big things I got lined up for you! I've been trying for two days—"

"I've been out of town," said Kilraine. "Just what is this job?"

"Can't talk now, Larry. Know anyone named Mike Wurzle?"

Kilraine started slightly. "I've heard of him."

"He'll be at your office to see you at four this afternoon. I'll come a little later to see how you make out. It's big, Larry, big!"

"Is Mike a friend of yours?"

"No. A friend of mine is sending him—Stern, a lawyer. Suit you?"

"Yes."

Kilraine put the instrument on its rack. His features changed: the strained look went out of them. Age fell from them. He glanced at Harmer, read the latter's expression of horror, and with a shrug reached for a cigarette from the open box on his desk.

"JOHN, THIS is beyond words!" broke out the lawyer. "Your face—"

"Harmer, I'm a man, not a boy," said Cabot crisply, and leaned back in his chair. "I handle my face as you might a bit of putty. In prison, I perfected that art, as I perfected what you choose to call my cheap magic.

"As Kilraine, ex-convict, I got to know a good many criminals. If I desire to put my talents and knowledge to work, not selfishly, but in the interests of society—"

"In common with a woman like this Viola Le May?" Harmer gestured in irritated negation. "A woman who'll drag you into the gutter? Bah!"

Cabot's mobile features hardened. "While I was in prison, this woman worked for me, Harmer. She lined up connections

"I never dreamed that I could be so glad to have a woman look after my interests," said Cabot gravely.

in the underworld for me. A real friend, unselfish, and according to her lights—"

"Is she in love with you, John?" asked the lawyer.

Cabot met his keen gaze, then broke into a little laugh.

"Don't be absurd. Business, gratitude, friendship, yes. Sentiment? No!"

Harmer's face was angry, but he repressed his emotion.

"I'll say no more. I came here on business, John. Before Mary Sargent took over the management of the estate, we got well shaken down by a new racket. On the Cabot Arms."

Cabot nodded. "The finest apartment building in the city. What about it?"

"Protection racket. We were forced to pay a thousand a month, after one terrible week when gas bombs were thrown, every window in the building smashed, and so forth. When you took over, the payments ceased. A man named Stern will probably see you about it."

"Stern!" Cabot's brows lifted. "Who is he?"

"A lawyer. Smooth, clever; you can't touch him. For two years the bar association has tried to get something on him and get him disbarred. Impossible. His clients, I gather, are some of the old beer racketeers, turning their talents to new fields because of the change in prohibition laws. There are many great estates in this city, funded properties, corporations founded on buildings and real estates. These are the victims of this new racket. Nor does it stop at murder."

"The Cabot Arms is protected by a private firm."

"One of whose operatives was killed at the entrance of the building. Shot down."

"Are you serious?" John Cabot stared at the older man. "I never heard of it!"

"You were still in prison when it happened."

THE SPEAKER on the desk buzzed. Cabot leaned forward. "Well?"

"A Mr. Stern is here to see you, Mr. Cabot," came the voice of Mary Sargent.

"Ask him to wait." Cabot straightened up. "Stern's here now. Shall I fight him?"

"No!" cried Harmer anxiously. "The Worthington people fought. It cost them a hundred thousand, two men killed, others hurt. Now, they pay promptly. I wanted to warn you. John. Later, we may find some way to checkmate these wolves, but—"

Cabot rose, put out his hand to the other in a warm grip.

"Harmer, I have to thank you for a lot. Don't worry about this affair. And don't worry about Kilraine. He'll not appear in this building again."

The lawyer shrugged, half angrily, and departed by the corridor.

Stern was a quiet, thin man of forty, well-dressed. His features were edged. His head, like that of Robespierre, was wedge-shaped; his eyes were bright, very alert. Pleasant in manner, he shook hands cordially and accepted a chair and a cigarette.

"Mr. Cabot, I want to see you about protection for your estate buildings, chiefly the Cabot Arms. What with unemployment and socialism, this city contains a large number of hoodlums—"

For three minutes he talked suavely, convincingly, earnestly. John Cabot perceived that Harmer was right, this man had brains; more brains, in a certain way, than all the bar association put together. Then Cabot intervened suddenly.

"One minute, Stern." He leaned back and smiled. "Scram!"

"Eh?" The other frowned, taken by surprise. "I don't understand—"

"You should. *Scram!*" Cabot reached out to the speaker on his desk. "Miss Sargent! Kindly call the officer from the downstairs hall to eject this rascal Stern—oh, never mind." He glanced up as Stern rose, white with fury. "Leaving, are you?"

"Yes," snapped Stern. "Here's my card, if you change your mind."

John Cabot reached out, picked up the card, tore it across,

and dropped it. Stern departed without another word. After a moment Mary Sargent knocked and entered.

"To judge by his face," she commented, "he didn't like the interview. Mr. Harmer was telling me about him when we were interrupted by those police. You mean to fight?"

Cabot rose, held the chair recently vacated by Stern, and beckoned.

"Here, young lady. I want to talk with you. Settle down and nerve yourself."

"That goes double," she said, after he had taken his own chair again.

"All right; shoot! I merely want you to talk, so pick your own topic and I'll listen."

She did not respond to his smile, but sat, regarding him with her poised, unafraid eyes, critically, almost challengingly. Abruptly, she spoke.

"As children, we played together. You've been away for years.

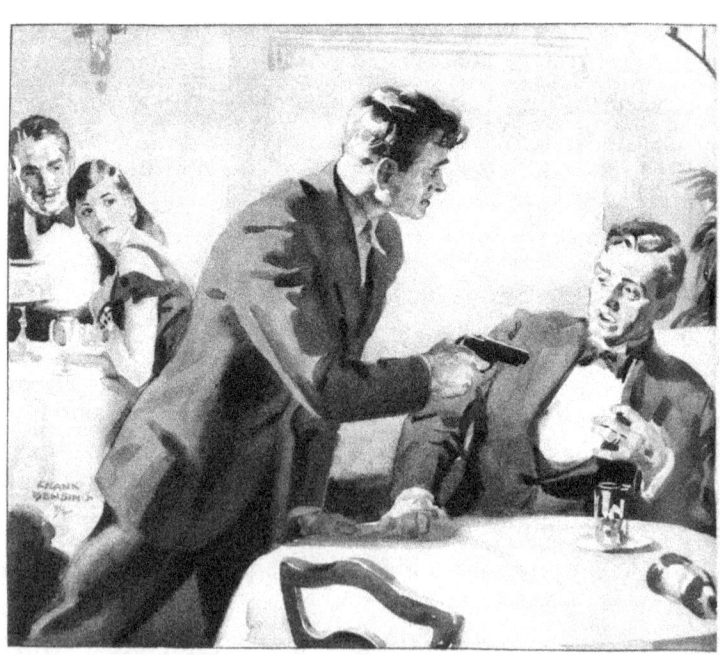

I'm now your secretary and manager of the estate. My job is to look out for your interests in every way."

"Conceded," said Cabot gravely. "I never dreamed that I could be so glad to have a woman look after my interest."

Under his gaze a little color rose in her cheeks, but her eyes did not falter.

"Twice I've seen this man Kilraine. You say he's an old friend to whom your private office is open at all times. Frequently, a woman has called him. I've listened in to their talk. A woman named Viola."

Cabot nodded, his eyes sharp. "Viola Le May. I know her."

"They spoke this morning. You must have hid the man here. They mentioned this fellow Stern," she said. "Look out for them, I warn you! The man those officers were after—I believe he's Kilraine! At the time of the Carias killing, I read his description in the paper. It fitted him."

"So I thought, myself," agreed Cabot. "Decidedly, he must change his clothes."

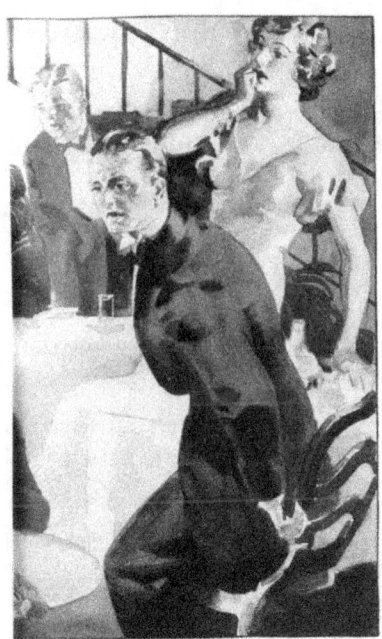

Her eyes dilated. "The man Kilraine was here this morning. Did you hide him, somehow?"

"Yes," said Cabot simply. "I'm under obligations to him. I don't like him, really. He's merely a necessary nuisance."

"Crossed us, did you? Well, take it yourself and see how you like it—"
There was the roaring explosion of a gun.

"Oh, it's so absurd for a man like you to speak that way!" she broke out. "To have such associates—you're so different from one of his type!"

"He'll not come here again, I promise you. On one condition."

"Yes? What it is?"

"That you abandon further work, discussion and business, and lunch with me."

"Cheap at the price!" she exclaimed, and laughing, came to her feet.

MIKE WURZLE fingered an unlit cigar. He was well-dressed, sleek, boldly handsome. His dark eyes expressed a consuming self-confidence, an arrogant disdain for all the world. His rather thick lips and heavy jaw revealed grossness, passion, cruelty.

"Now get this," he pursued easily. "Stern slipped me the word. We've looked you up and you're oke with us. You heard about me when you was in stir, huh? French Johnny told you? He's in my mob now. He says you're oke. But you got to show us.

"You go along with us tonight. We'll do the job, see? Then, we'll go on to the Dixie Club, you and me. Stern's throwing a party there tonight. You'll meet him and get paid, see?"

"I see," said Kilraine in a low voice, gazing intently at the other. "Did you ever hear of a radio brain, Mike?"

"Hell, no. Is it some joke?"

Kilraine smiled thinly.

"Listen; I can tell you what's passing in that brain of yours, some of it. In other brains, perhaps. This job tonight! Your last job, Mike. Chicago. The Midway Hotel—"

"Holy smoke!" ejaculated the other. His eyes dilated. In them darted fear, anger, amazement, terror.

Kilraine went on calmly.

"The Cabot Arms; that's tonight's job. Right? Others are in it. I get three names. French Johnny; Ceccolini; Lefty Quinn.

Quinn! You say he's the man who shot down that radio car officer last week?"

Mike Wurzle shrank suddenly. Then he burst out in violent, gusty words.

"You're a liar; I didn't say so! I never said so! Anyhow, he was drunk then—"

"Twenty grand. Midway Hotel. Twenty grand!" went on Kilraine slowly. The sleek features of Wurzle showed tiny drops of perspiration starting on brow and cheeks. Pallor crept into that high-boned, arrogant face. "You're afraid of something, of some one, here—"

A swift, savage contortion twisted Wurzle's lips. He reached out, caught Kilraine by the wrist, and glared at him. His hoarse voice came pantingly.

"Stop it, you devil! Magician, huh? Korvo the Great, huh? Well, don't pull no more of that stuff on me. Afraid? I ain't afraid of nobody, see? Nobody!" He fell silent, breathing heavily, then calmed down before the quiet smile of Kilraine. "It's true, buddy," he went on, with a curt nod. "I'm all washed up with this town. I'm blowing to Chi tomorrow; and nobody else knows. I'll start on my own racket there."

"Apparently, I know what I'm talking about, eh?"

Wurzle darted him a quick glance, looked away, and nodded.

"I see you're telling the truth." Kilraine produced cigarettes, lit one, and lessened the tension. "Now, old man, forget about all this. What passes between us is nobody's business. You'll come for me tonight?"

"Yeah; nine sharp. I'll honk for you outside here. Wear the soup and fish, see? On account of the Dixie Club afterward. Nothing to this Cabot Arms job. It's a pipe."

"I happen to know that two private detectives were hired today to guard that building."

"Yeah?" Wurzle's eyes hardened into black agate. "Fair enough. We been waiting to get some of them private dicks! We'll knock off the both of 'em, just for a lesson. See you later."

Kilraine nodded. Mike Wurzle stumbled to his feet, mopped his face, and departed.

After a moment Kilraine reached to the lower shelf of the table and brought out a desk telephone. He dialed a number, and, presently, spoke in the voice of Cabot.

"Hello, Harmer! John Cabot speaking. I want you to do something for me, with no protests. At eight-thirty tonight, get into touch with the police. Got a pencil? Take these names. Mike Wurzle, French Johnny, ex-convict, Ceccolini. Lefty Quinn. Quinn is the bird who shot that radio car officer last week. A few minutes after nine, they're coming to bomb the Cabot Arms with the deliberate intent of killing the two private dicks who are guarding the building. Tell the police to shoot first and shoot fast—"

He hung up. Barely had he replaced the instrument, than a tap sounded at the door. Rising, Kilraine crossed the room and admitted Viola Le May.

"L A R R Y ! I T ' S sure good to see you—been out of town, eh?" she exclaimed with impulsive cordiality. Indeed, she seemed about to take him in her arms; but Kilraine laughed and waved his cigarette toward a chair. He quite ignored her exotic loveliness, the eager appeal of her great dark eyes, and calmly returned to his own seat.

"Well, Mike Wurzle was just here," he observed.

"Oh!" She sank into the chair opposite, and her gaze widened on him. "Did it come off all right?"

"Quite, thanks. I presume I have you to thank?"

"Sure. I got the lawyer Stern on the string—can't quite shake him, either," and she laughed rather nervously. "He's the big shot in this town, Larry; he can do anything! He thinks you're a relative of mine. He's giving a party for me tonight."

"That's right. You're singing at the Dixie Club, aren't you?"

She nodded excitedly. "Larry, I'm thrilled to death about it! If you click with Stern, then it's a pipe! I've got it all framed up for you. He'll put you right into the big money as soon as he's satisfied you're the man for him."

"You think he runs things? Well, let that pass." Kilraine regarded her curiously. "Viola, I thought you had my best interests at heart."

She gave him a blanky startled look. "What's the big idea, Larry? You know I'd do anything for you."

"Well," cut in Kilraine quickly, "why do you wish me in on a racket that means extortion, wreckage, murder?"

"Oh! You've got it all wrong, Larry." Her eyes glistened on him; pride was in them, confidence, perhaps deeper emotions. "You won't be doing that end of it for any time. You're going over big, right into the big money, Larry! I've got it fixed with Stern. As for the racket itself, what of it?" and she shrugged lightly.

"It's only squeezing money out of these corporations and big estates. They can afford it. They ought to pay, and pay big! They squeeze the poor devils under them."

Kilraine broke into a laugh. "Well, tell me something! You know this fellow Wurzle, I presume. Has he any connection with a woman called Blaney? Nell Blaney? That's the name I seemed to get, but I can't be sure."

She caught her breath sharply. "Larry, you're certainly the devil himself! Give me a smoke. Thanks." She leaned back in her chair, inhaled, and nodded at him.

"Nell was Stern's girl, see? Stern was mad about her and still is. She's all hepped up about Wurzle; crazy about him! Stern doesn't know that she skipped out yesterday and went to Chicago, with her clothes and jewels. The joke is that she's going to meet Wurzle there."

Kilraine's black brows drew down sharply. "And how the devil do you know all this?"

"Nell told me." Viola waved her cigarette gaily. "She lives, or lived, right across the hall from me, see? Well, she thinks I want to take her place with Stern. And Stern doesn't know yet that she's skipped out on him! Thinks she's at Atlantic City. Ain't that rich?"

Kilraine whistled softly. Then, beneath his kindling eyes, a thin, cruel smile curved his lips.

NINE O'CLOCK. Down the dark street, prompt to the minute, came a large car and halted beneath the windows of Kilraine's dingy apartment. The horn sounded imperatively.

Kilraine, a light overcoat cloaking his stooping figure, left the entrance and approached the car. Four figures gathered about him on the sidewalk.

"Hi, there!" exclaimed Mike Wurzle cordially. "Kilraine, you know French Johnny already. This here is Tony Ceccolini. This is Lefty Quinn. Pile in, everybody. Make it snappy."

"Hold on!" exclaimed Kilraine, as they turned to the car. "You'll have to go without me, boys. I just got a telephone message from Stern. Wants me to come right down to the Dixie Club and meet him. He says for you to go on to the Cabot Arms, and he'll send you special orders by me—"

There was a sudden silence, an immobility; Kilraine, who had counted on leaving the four with breezy, negligent assurance, slowly became aware of his frightful error. Then, as by tacit consent, the four men moved, closed around him. Something hard, in Quinn's hand, was rammed into his stomach.

"Yellow, are you?" snarled Quinn.

But Frenchy cut in abruptly, anxiously. "Aw, he ain't yeller, Lefty! Maybe Stern did give orders—"

"Like hell!" snapped Wurzle. "I'm giving orders, see? Get in. Quinn, you drive! I'll settle this on the way."

Kilraine was violently shoved into the rear of the car, Wurzle holding his arm. French Johnny and Ceccolini were crowded beside him. He was helpless, unable to move. Next minute the car was moving into speed.

A black limousine, that had been standing in the middle of the block, came into sudden life. It purred after the car, keeping cautious distance. Kilraine glimpsed its lights as they turned the corner. Bowker was following, then—Bowker, his chauffeur, the one man he could trust with his secret! A good man. Bowker, who had followed Larry Kilraine out of prison, with dog-like devotion.

"What's all this bunk, now?" Mike Wurzle was growling, giving Kilraine's arm a vicious twist. "Who gave you this telephone message?"

"Stern himself. Not five minutes ago."

"You lie. He don't give orders that way. You're yellow and want to quit on us, huh? Not much. We'll be there in a minute, now. Lefty! Stop the car just before reaching the joint. Leave the engine going. You handle the tommy gun on them dicks. The rest of us, slather every window in sight. Kilraine, these are glass pineapples, so watch out—"

Kilraine felt small, cold spheres pressed into his hands. The car roared on, then slowed down. A block away appeared the brightly lighted facade of Cabot Arms. Cars lined the curb throughout the block.

"Double park, Lefty," ordered Wurzle. "Hey, Kilraine! Feeling nervous, huh?"

"Not as nervous as you'll feel," said Kilraine. "That message said that Stern knew all about Nell Blaney going to Chicago, and who she meant to meet there."

THE OTHER exploded in an oath of astounded incredulity.

"What? Say, if that rat Stern has double-crossed us—"

The car halted outside the line of parked vehicles. Lefty Quinn alighted, a sub-machine gun under his arm.

"Pile out, pile out!" he snapped. "What's got into you guys? Get it over with!"

Kilraine was shoved out by Wurzle, who was still cursing fluently. All five men ducked between the standing cars to the sidewalk, and started toward the canopied entrance. The front of the Cabot Arms, on either side the entrance, was masked by small trees and shrubs. As Quinn, in the lead, nearly reached the canopy, a voice came leaping from this leafy cover, beside them.

"You're covered, boys. Stick 'em up—"

From beneath Quinn's arm darted roaring fire. A scream rang out. Then, red jets, flaming pistols, roaring shots, from every side. Police whistles. A dozen figures darted into sight, ahead, behind. Bullets tore through the parked cars. Quinn was sprawled on the curb. Ceccolini, firing and cursing, fell on top of him. Bullets riddled French Johnny.

At the first voice, Kilraine tossed away his bombs and dropped headlong. He rolled off the sidewalk, under the car that stood against the curb. He scrambled out on the far side of it as the inferno broke loose, and gained his feet. He was running frantically, back along the line of cars. Bullets showered around. Police were across the street shooting, running, pursuing.

He ducked around Wurzle's car, then cut in close to the house fronts. They had seen him, were after him! More bullets. Staccato firing volleyed up the sky. One struck. He felt the impact, the jerk of it, but kept going. Kilraine, ex-convict! Nothing could save him now if they caught him. Nothing!

Ahead, at the corner, a large car was turning about. His own car! Bowker was turning, ready for flight. No! The car halted. Kilraine spurted desperately. A sub-machine gun shattered the night. A bullet went between arm and side, gashing open his clothes, but merely burning his skin. Then he was at the car, gasping, reeling. A door swung open. He hurled himself in. With one roaring leap, the car spurted away.

FOR A moment Kilraine lay back on the cushions. He was flung off balance as the big car reeled around corners, careened madly from one street to the next. Then the speed lessened. Kilraine sat up and caught at the speaking tube.

"Bowker? Thanks, old man. Great work! Drive around a bit, for ten minutes, then stop at the Dixie Club."

"Right, sir."

Kilraine pulled down the blinds, switched on the overhead

light. A panel swung open to his touch, a drawer slid out. At his feet was a bag. He opened it painfully, then got out of his ripped smoking jacket. Blood was running down over his left hand. He opened the shirt sleeve; by a miracle, no blood was on the cuff. The flesh of his upper arm, above the elbow, was torn and mangled, spouting blood. No dark blood; no cut artery, luckily.

"Missed the bone. No great damage," muttered Kilraine. "The shirt can remain."

He worked fast. The fiery sting of iodine drew a grunt from him. A compress, a bandage, adhesive tape; all accomplished in three minutes. The fingers of Korvo the Great were deft, practiced, marvelous.

Now the black tie was jerked off. A mirror opened into sight. His felt hat was tossed aside. The black brows of Kilraine became brown; the grayish pallor was wiped from his face. The face of John Cabot evolved from those strained, haggard features.

A white tie—yes, he could use his left hand, although it hurt. White waistcoat and evening coat from the grip. Only an effort, sharp with pain, got him into the coat; then he relaxed. From his shoes he snapped the false heels that gave Kilraine height. An opera hat leaped out into full shape as he touched the spring. Then he jammed everything into the grip, closed the panel and drawer, slid back the mirror.

The car halted before the Dixie Club. John Cabot alighted, impeccable as usual, and paused to light a cigarette.

"Better wait, Bowker; I may not be long," he said. "Then we'll go to Mr. Harmer's house. By the way, your tail-light isn't working."

"I'll fix it at once, sir." Bowker stifled a grin as he saluted. Trust him to see that the police did not get his number!

John Cabot entered the place, left his hat and a smiling word with the check girl, and passed on to the lower level of the floor. The Dixie Club was large, garish, popular. The cabaret had finished for the moment, and dancers crowded the oblong of floor. Cabot beckoned the manager, who recognized him and came to the foot of the stairs.

"Ah, Mr. Cabot! Alone this evening? Or looking for some-one?"

"Get me a table, please," said Cabot. "Mr. Stern is here, I think?"

"Oh, yes, sir! A table near his?"

"Anywhere. Then ask him to come to my table at once that I want to speak with him—"

They both turned abruptly, at an outburst of angry excla-mations from the entry. Down the steps leaped a wild figure, directly at them, thrusting them both aside with an oath. It was Mike Wurzle, hatless, blood on his cheek, coat half-torn away, a pistol in his hand. He dived into the crowd ahead.

Shrill voices rose. Then lifted Wurzle's voice, deadly, piercing.

"You damned rat: Crossed us, did you? Turned us in—well, take it yourself! See how you like it—"

The roaring explosion of a pistol smashed out. Another, another. Frantic shrieks, yells, screams, a tumult of figures. Then past Cabot hurtled a police officer, others following pandemo-nium!

Presently, Cabot gained the outside sidewalk amid a stream of figures. Almost beside him came a woman's voice, one that he recognized.

"My God! That officer shot him like a dog—let's get away, quick, before they hold us! Did you see Stern's face after those bullets went into him? Got out of the way, you!"

It was Viola Le May, another girl clinging to her arm. She shoved Cabot aside with one impatient glance and hurried on. John Cabot edged out of the throng and passed on down the sidewalk to where his limousine waited. Bowker held open the door.

"Any trouble, Bowker?"

"None whatever, sir. What happened in there?"

"A mistake, I'm afraid."

"To Mr. Harmer's house, sir?"

Cabot laughed shortly as he got in. "No; not tonight. Not even a magician can get ahead of the devil! Drive home."

THE MAN WITH THE RUBBER FACE

ANOTHER ASTOUNDING ADVENTURE OF JOHN CABOT, WHO
COULD CHANGE HIS IDENTITY AT WILL, AND WHO USED HIS
UNCANNY POWERS IN A PRIVATE WAR ON THE UNDERWORLD.

IN AN upper room of the old Cabot mansion, John Cabot stood putting the finishing touches to his attire for the evening. It was seven-thirty.

"Not a bad bow, Watson," he said to his attentive valet. "I suppose the guests will be along at any minute. Everything ready downstairs?"

"Quite, sir," assented Watson. He turned as the telephone bell jangled.

"Mr. Harmer, sir."

John Cabot took the instrument. Harmer, the family lawyer! Harmer, one of two men who knew his secret and whom he could trust implicitly!

"Evening, John," came the lawyer's voice. "I'm frightfully sorry to say that I can't show up at your party. I've just been talking with Washington, and must catch the eight o'clock express. And, John! There's something I must tell you. The killer of Ben Carias, and the one man of the Wurzle gang who escaped, has been identified by the police."

"Yes?" Cabot's voice was calm, despite the icy constriction of his heart. "Who?"

"An ex-convict named Kilraine. Goodnight, John. I'll see you the minute I return."

Cabot swung around. "Watson, send Bowker here at once. Leave us alone."

The valet disappeared. John Cabot stared into his mirrored

reflection, and wondered that his face was not pale. So they knew now that this man was Larry Kilraine!

Luckily, they did not know, never would know, that Larry Kilraine was John Cabot.

Bowker arrived, bull-necked, sturdy, devoted. He was the second man John Cabot could trust. Bowker had left jail at the same time Larry Kilraine was freed, and had become Cabot's chauffeur. He knew that John Cabot had earned a living as a professional magician, under the name of Kilraine, alias Korvo the Great; and he knew much more besides.

"Bowker," said Cabot curtly, "they know that it was Kilraine who killed Ben Carias."

Bowker grunted. "But you didn't, sir!"

"No matter. The police are out after Kilraine, or will be soon. As far as I'm concerned Kilraine must be dead, wiped out forever." Cabot was decisive, spurred by crisis. "But there are some things at Kilraine's apartment I must get; clothes, make-up stuff, things I couldn't replace. And I left my own coat there last time I was at the place. Might be traced to me through my tailor."

"I'll get the stuff," volunteered Bowker quickly. Cabot clapped him on the shoulder.

"You will not! It's my job. They're not likely to be watching the place yet; I'll chance it. Let's see; the dancing begins at ten. I must be here for the first dance. Immediately that's over, I'll come out to the side entrance. Be there with the car."

N O N E   O F the thronging guests who greeted the bronzed, smiling John Cabot, could guess the mingled apprehension and relief that lay behind his dark eyes. But apprehension died, and relief grew. Now that he was forced to it, let Kilraine be dead forever and good riddance! Kilraine, ex-convict, magician, had turned in many a crook; the police and the underworld alike were undoubtedly on his trail now. And the mysterious Big Shot, the unknown person who controlled the underworld of the city and state, was a bad enemy.

The guests trooped in. This was the first time the old Cabot mansion had been thrown open since John Cabot came home from Africa (presumably) to take over his inheritance. Old friends of the family, social leaders of the city, financiers; curiosity, and a keen interest in the heir, brought them, for few had seen John Cabot since he was a boy.

A simple dinner dance—but even to these guests of position, wealth, culture, the setting was impressive. John Cabot had modernized the old house, yet it still bore the magnificent traces of three past generations.

At the great dining room table were gathered a score of guests who had in other days been particular friends of the family. Opposite Cabot, at the table's foot, sat Mary Sargent, now his secretary and manager of the Cabot estate. At his left was her uncle, Winthrop Blake, famous attorney and at present police commissioner of the city. Handsome, urbane, distinguished. Winthrop Blake was already mentioned as the next governor of the state.

Otherwise, this table held older faces. The dowager Astorbilt, on Cabot's right hand. Bishop Lane, severe, ascetic spiritual

"My dear," said Cabot gravely, "I promise not to have anything more to do with Kilraine."

leader. Mrs. Grace Macey, for twenty years undisputed social arbiter of the fast dwindling Four Hundred. Fulton Perkins, sportsman and millionaire, friend of kings.

Looking down the long table to the smiling beauty of Mary Sargent, Cabot felt his heart leap at the sight of her there. He groped at a dim vision of the future; then a chill gust of fear banished it all. She, at least, must never know! To her, Kilraine must be no more than an unpleasant character.

"John!" Winthrop Blake was leaning over, speaking softly. "I want a word with you in private when this breaks up. Rather important."

"Right," said Cabot. "Before we go upstairs to dance, eh? I'll see you in the library."

Mrs. Astorbilt demanded his attention; but through the polite words and light chatter, Cabot occasionally glanced at the strong, dominant profile of Blake. Power in those handsome features, and a touch of cruelty as well.

SO THE dinner passed. Presently, Cabot was ushering Winthrop Blake into the library, unchanged in any detail for a generation past. He set out cigars. Blake took one, lit it, and then gave his host a keen look.

"Cabot, this city is being purged by crime; and I mean just that. Criminals are everywhere, are getting away with jobs on every hand; we can't check 'em. Now, I want to warn you that you have one in your employ. A man named Bowker, an ex-convict."

Cabot nodded coolly. "I'm aware of it. I know Bowker's story. I believe he'll make good if given a chance."

Blake's face cleared. "Good for you! You know, I was afraid you might not know his record. Look here, John! This was reported to me; you know they keep a record of all ex-convicts. If you'd like to help this man Bowker, and will give me a line to the effect that he's making good with you, it'll bring him a good mark—eh?"

"With all my heart!" exclaimed Cabot, and crossed to the

desk. The police commissioner followed, drawing an envelope from his pocket.

"Here, use this—official stationery, to give it weight. And my pen; it holds ink that can't be altered. My pet invention and hobby. Drop down to my office one of these days, and you'll find some of these things vastly interesting, even to an idle young devil like yourself!"

"I'll do just that," assented Cabot. "Damn! Your pen may be elegant, but it leaks ink—well, never mind."

He took a blank sheet of Blake's official stationery from the envelope, and upon it scrawled a note to the effect that Bowker was serving him well and honestly, and gave every evidence of going straight and reforming. Then he came hastily to his feet.

"There you are, Blake—good Lord! I've got the first dance with Mary, and wouldn't miss it for the world! See you later. Excuse me if I run."

He departed hurriedly. Blake glanced after him, then leaned over the desk. The note, he folded and replaced in its envelope. The fountain pen, he closed very carefully, then wrapped it in his silk handkerchief, careless of ink stains, and pocketed it with the envelope.

His brows lifted quizzically.

"And they said he was a smart one!" he muttered.

JOHN CABOT danced with Mary Sargent; his duty as host was over, and he was free to be himself for the rest of the evening.

"John, it's perfect—all of it!" she murmured. "I wasn't made for poverty, for living on the bounty of my unclc. I'm glad that I'm self-supporting now. I love all this glitter, this music—I can appreciate it."

"You darling!" exclaimed Cabot. "Well, that's what you are, so no objections. Eh? And why the sudden frown?"

She broke into quick laughter. "Nothing. We'll not intrude it on this perfect evening—"

Small plugs of cotton spread out his nostrils;
slowly, a different, coarser face appeared.

She halted him swiftly. "All right, if you must know, I was thinking about that awful man whom I dislike so heartily."

"Oh! Kilraine!" said Cabot. "He's banished forever."

She looked at him suddenly, straight in the eyes.

"John Cabot! Do you mean that? Are you serious?"

"Absolutely. He'll never come into the office again. I'll never see him again or have anything to do with him. Word of honor."

He felt the quick pressure of her fingers on his shoulder. Her eyes shone warmly.

"Good! You make me happy, delighted! Thanks, John."

The music ceased.

Five minutes later, Cabot emerged from the side door. Under the *porte-cochère* stood a black limousine, the door open. He plunged in, slammed the door, and picked up the speaking tube as the car started.

"Take it easy, Bowker; I had no time to change," he said, then fell to work.

He snapped down the blinds, switched on the overhead light. A panel slipped away to disclose a hidden recess; a drawer slid out, a mirror appeared at his touch. Here were all the appurtenances of a dressing-room, suddenly in sight. Throwing off his dress coat, Cabot drew over his head a blue denim blouse that came up high around his throat and concealed his shirt and collar, then drew a dirty, frayed cap tightly over his head.

He stared into the mirror. And as he stared, his face changed.

The regular features altered with a steady, horrifying certitude, as his head sank down between his shoulders. A wolfish snarl drew his lips aside; his brows came down, his fine nostrils thickened. A natural command of facial muscles, brought to awful perfection by days and weeks of practice behind prison bars—such patient, unrelenting practice as only one trained to the magician's art could encompass.

With a nod of satisfaction, Cabot reached into a box. His swift, sure fingers rolled plugs of cotton; these spread out his nostrils, thickened his lips, aided the changes caused by muscular action and relieved the nervous tension. A different, coarse face appeared. A dust of black powder across the brown eyebrows, a quick, deft smear of dirt over jaws and cheeks, formed the only touch of make-up. The car slowed, came to a halt.

"Looks clear, sir," said Bowker, "But I got a queer feeling."

"So have I," said Cabot grimly. "Keep the engine running."

HE TURNED to the dingy apartment building that housed the office of Kilraine, took the keys from his pocket, and entered. Inside, seeing no one, he passed to the corner apartment, opened its door, and switched on the light.

He halted abruptly. Nearly two weeks since he had been here; but upon the air hung the scent of tobacco. Cigars. His dark eyes glinted around in startled probing. The central room was almost empty, black drapes, touched with scarlet, covered the walls and doors. A large framed poster of Korvo the Great alone broke the ominous expanse. A table in the window bore a crystal ball on its stand; on the lower shelf was a telephone.

To the left, behind those drapes, was a small kitchen, nothing more. To the right opened the bedroom with its cot and the things he had come here to get. He hesitated, then turned to it, thrust aside the drapes, looked between two heavy sliding doors.

Empty.

He entered this room, found the coat he had left here, carelessly—too carelessly!—lying on a chair. Crossing to a large closet, he opened it, thrust aside garments that hung on a pole, and revealed a very unsuspected door. This was locked. He put a key in the lock, turned it, and left it so.

From the closet he took a large bag and into it thrust the coat, following this with boxes, small articles, pulled hurriedly from drawers and shelves. A glance around, then he closed the bag and thrust it into the closet. He came back to the sliding doors and pulled them nearly shut, then stepped into the central, black-hung room. An instant he stood there, irresolute.

"Nonsense! No danger here now," he murmured, and crossed

to the table, letting the drapes fall behind him. He seated himself, picked up the telephone, called a number.

"HELLO, VIOLA!" he exclaimed in the throaty, rather husky voice of Kilraine.

"Larry!" came the glad cry. He smiled grimly as the voice babbled on. He had picked Viola Le May from the streets, trained her as his assistant, aided her to become the sort of woman she had vainly dreamed. While he was in prison, she had become a cabaret singer, widening her acquaintance, lining up jobs for him—the kind of jobs an ex-convict would jump at. Little she knew that Kilraine had become John Cabot!

"Listen, Viola," he broke in abruptly. "I've got bad news for you. The bulls are wise; they're after me for killing Ben Carias and for other jobs. They're out after me. If they get me, it's the chair or the big house for life. I'm off tonight for the Coast, understand? And the Big Shot is after me, from the other side. Every crook in town is looking for me, too—"

"Oh, Larry!" At her cry, at the swift anguish in her voice, Cabot started. But he gave her no time to go on.

"Snap out of it," he pursued quickly. "I'll communicate with you. A man named Mark Lemon. Remember the name, Mark Lemon! You can trust him. Or else Bowker may come—you know Bowker! But I'm on the lam—"

"Wait, Larry!" she broke in desperately, urgently. "I've got something here for you, something that came only yesterday for you. It's big. Larry! You'll need it. You must get it—"

"Good Lord! I'm on my way to the station now!" he exclaimed impatiently.

"No matter. Come here, send, but get it! Just a small package. It's your share of the Templehof job; a messenger left it. I looked into it. It's wonderful, Larry! You must get it, take it with you—"

Templehof! Cabot frowned; he knew of no such job, had not the ghost of an idea what she meant, but he knew that Viola Le May could be trusted. His face cleared.

"I'll have Bowker get it in a few minutes and bring it to me," he said rapidly. "Now, listen! Too many people know we've been associated; it'll be dangerous for you. Give out word tonight, somehow, that we've broken off, that I've left town and you never want to see me again. For your own sake, understand?"

"Yes, Larry." A sob now. Cabot swore under his breath. He had not suspected this, had not thought of sentiment in their relations. "When will I see you, Larry? Will you let me know?"

"When it's safe," he said abruptly, and hung up. He cursed himself for a brute, but he had no choice in the matter.

Rising, he started toward the bedroom. Then, just as he put out his hand to the drapes, he stiffened.

"Up!" came a voice. "Up, Kilraine!"

His head turned. Ghastly despair seized upon him. They had been hidden in the kitchen all the time. Now they were out, coming toward him; two detectives, pistols ready, eyes grimly promising to use those pistols. They were dealing with a killer.

"MISS LE May's apartment, Bowker. Stop half a block from there, go on afoot. Say that Kilraine sent you for a package; you'll take it down to the station and meet Kilraine. He's leaving in half-an-hour for Los Angeles. Don't let her come, on any account. Get me?"

"Got you," came the curt response.

Unhurried now, Cabot got rid of the blouse. He let his features return to their natural lines, inspected his attire, straightened his tie. Cold cream and a towel cleansed his face. He was getting into his dress coat when the car halted.

Himself again, Cabot put up the blinds, lit a cigarette and settled back to wait. It was not long until Bowker appeared, his heavy figure trim in its whipcord uniform, a small package in his hand. He ducked directly under the wheel and drove the car away.

"Keep a lookout, sir," came his voice. "Ain't sure, but seemed to me like too many birds was hanging around that joint. She said to tell you good luck, and this came to her for you from somebody you knew in Washington. She was crying and all broke up."

Washington! Templehof! Cabot's brain raced, but to no avail, as he glanced back. He saw nothing suspicious. Bowker passed back the package. This was apparently a small box, and under the string that tied it was thrust an envelope, unaddressed. Cabot switched on the light and tore open the envelope.

In his hand dropped a hundred-dollar bill, and a scrap of paper, hastily scrawled:

"Larry:
    You may need this worse than I do. Take it, old pal, and good luck. God bless you.
                            Viola."

Twenty minutes later. John Cabot was once more moving among his guests, his absence unobserved by any.

By two o'clock the last guest had departed. The ballroom was empty and dark, and Cabot, retiring, dismissed his valet. Alone in his bedroom, he got out of his coat, slipped into a dressing-gown, and produced the package that Viola Le May had sent to Kilraine. He cut the strings, laid bare a plain pasteboard box, and opened it.

Before him lay a blazing green mass of the most precious stones in the world—emeralds!

Cabot fingered them, incredulous. One glance told him they were not only real, but such emeralds as he had never seen in his life; enormous, pure, flawless. He looked at the settings. Necklaces, bracelets, pendants, of the most magnificent workmanship. Here was a fortune beside which Viola's hundred-dollar bill was like a postage stamp.

"But what the devil does it mean?" he muttered, staring.

The telephone jarred in upon his amazement. The telephone—after two in the morning!

"Hello!" he responded.

"John! This is Mary Sargent. I must see you instantly! I'm coming right over in my car." Her voice was urgent, breathless. He had never imagined that this calm, poised girl with the level eyes could be so excited. "Meet me at the side entrance." And rang off.

Wondering, perturbed Cabot thrust the astounding stones aside, got out of his dressing-gown, and donned hat and overcoat. Mary Sargent lived with the Blakes, only a few blocks distant. What had happened? Anything was possible. And at this hour of the morning, too?

Into his overcoat pocket,

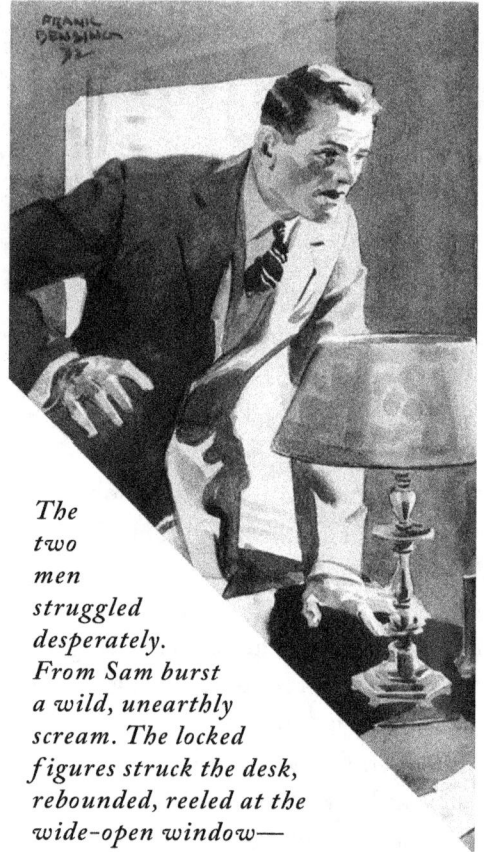

The two men struggled desperately. From Sam burst a wild, unearthly scream. The locked figures struck the desk, rebounded, reeled at the wide-open window—

Cabot thrust the pistol from his dresser drawer, and then descended through the dark and silent house to the side entrance. Beneath the *porte-cochère* he paused, and glanced back at the garage. A light showed in the upper room of this— Bowker lived there alone.

Then he turned as a small car came up the drive. He strode out to meet it in the circle at the side of the house, and a moment later stood beside Mary Sargent.

"Well, the surprise is joyful!" he said lightly. "Didn't you get enough party—"

"John! No nonsense," she broke in. He was astonished at sight of her urgent, wide-eyed face. "Uncle was talking as we drove home. He mentioned that the police have found out about Kilraine—that friend of yours! Understand? That he's a murderer, a killer! I had to let you know at once. In spite of your promise—"

"My dear," said Cabot gravely, "my promise holds. I found out about all this earlier today; Harmer learned it, and telephoned me. That's one reason I promised you not to have anything more to do with this Kilraine. I'm done with him. Unless vitally necessary to me, he'll never show up again; upon my word. He's gone to the Pacific Coast, has skipped out for good. Satisfied?"

She drew a deep breath.

"And to think of my coming over here—well, no matter. I'm glad you're rid of him."

"Me, too." Cabot opened the car door. "I'll drive you home and walk back; I insist. I need a walk to clear my head. My dear, it was good of you to come over, to warn me. I appreciate it with all my heart."

That was all, yet so much lay in his simple words that she was silent. Nor did he speak again until he was getting out of the car at her door.

"By the way, do you know anything about Washington?" he asked. "Have you heard anything about a jewel robbery there? Some one was talking about it. Templehof—"

"Templehof! Good heavens. John, don't you read the papers?" she exclaimed. "For three days they've been full of it. A broker or agent there had a lot of jewels they say the late King of Spain sent over here for sale. He was robbed, and the loss ran into huge figures. You'd better go to bed and read the papers tomorrow. Goodnight."

"Goodnight," said John Cabot, and walked home mechanically, like a man in a dream. What the devil could it all mean?

HE WAS letting himself in the door when he remembered Bowker, and going out to the drive, saw a light still in the chauffeur's room. He strode out to the garage. The man's quarters were reached by outside stairs, and as he began the ascent, Cabot heard a growling voice above. He paused, then ascended quietly. An oath came to him, and another.

Outside the door of Bowker's room, he halted, listening. A low cry reached him; a cry of pain. Then a voice.

"Come across, damn you! We mean business, you fool. Burn his feet some more, Pete! Come on, now, talk! Where's this Kilraine, huh? Where'd you put that package?"

Cabot's fingers closed on the pistol. He saw everything in a flash; they had followed the car here. The emeralds had been a plant—unknown to Viola! Kilraine had escaped the police on one hand, only to fall into a trap set by the underworld, by the Big Shot, that unknown person who—

Another cry of pain. Cabot reached out, silently opened the door. Before him sat Bowker, lashed in a chair, gagged, stubbornly shaking his head. Two men, their back to the door; one, kneeling, held matches to Bowker's naked feet. The other held a "sap", with which he must have been beating their victim.

"Stick 'em up!" snapped the hoarse voice of Kilraine.

The two flung a glance at the doorway. There, overcoat buttoned up close, hat pulled down, was the stoop-shouldered figure of Larry Kilraine. The dark eyes glared at them from his drawn, wolfish features; over the pistol, his face was drawn, snarling, frightful. Stupefied, the two men lifted their hands.

"Cut him loose, Pete! Move fast. Bowker, frisk 'em; stand 'em up."

The two frightened thugs lined up against the wall. Bowker, grimly intent with pistol and billy, said nothing. Kilraine came up close to them, said nothing, stared at them. After a moment, babbling words broke from them; pleas, oaths, whines.

"So!" said Kilraine abruptly. "What's his name, you—the man who sent you here? His name! The man who planted that package, set you to watch when I came for it!"

"Honest, Kilraine!" whined one. "Nobody knows his name. We don't. Maybe some guy here and there—it's the Big Shot, Kilraine! He don't tell nobody, see? Us mugs gets our orders—"

"I see you're not lying, anyhow," said Kilraine. "Bowker, want to beat 'em up?"

"To hell with them," snapped Bowker disgustedly. "I ain't hurt."

"All right." Kilraine turned to the pair. "Clear out. Tell the Big Shot that I'm going West tonight, see? But I'm coming back. And I'm coming back to get him! Scram!"

The two departed hastily.

EIGHT THE next morning. John Cabot, after dressing, slipped the pasteboard box of emeralds into his pocket and turned to his telephone. A moment later he had Winthrop Blake on the wire.

"Morning, commissioner!" he exclaimed cheerily. "Going to work today? I'd like the earliest possible appointment with you. It's rather important."

"Right, John," came the response. "Say, nine-thirty, at my office?"

"I'll be there," answered Cabot.

At nine-thirty to the minute, he was ushered into Blake's private office. No dingy police headquarters, but a great corner room high in a downtown building, overlooking the river. Still an athlete, despite the gray at his temples, Blake liked fresh air on these lively spring mornings, and the two big windows near his desk were flung wide open.

To Cabot's abrupt astonishment, Blake made no response to his greeting, but looked up at him with a singular expression and motioned toward a chair.

"Sit down, Cabot. Just a moment, till I examine these prints."

Before him were two slips of paper bearing finger-prints. He picked up an enlarging glass and continued a minute examination of the prints, evidently comparing the two sets. John Cabot, astounded by this reception, lit a cigarette and composed himself to wait. He was struck again by the harsh element in Winthrop Blake's handsome features, an element of cruelty, of ruthlessness.

Then, suddenly, Blake laid aside the glass, leaned back in his chair, gazed at Cabot.

"Glad you came: saved me the trouble of sending for you," he said abruptly. "Before you took over the family estate, I believe you were in Africa?"

Cabot nodded. "Africa and parts adjacent. I supported myself in those days."

"As a magician, perhaps?"

The attack was cold, hard, impersonal. Cabot tingled to a sudden sense of peril. This man. Mary Sargent's uncle, a family friend—

"Just what do you mean, Blake?" he queried.

"I mean that you're caught," said Winthrop Blake, unsmiling. "When the police nearly grabbed the murderer of Ben Carias, he vanished in or around your office. Yesterday, this man was identified as Kilraine. I looked up Kilraine. He got out of jail shortly before you appeared here, after some years of wandering. Bowker and Kilraine were pals in prison. You see the inference."

"Rather, coincidence," murmured Cabot.

At first stupefied, shocked into chill horror, now he wakened. His brain leaped to the alert. He settled himself to fight.

"No," said Blake, his eyes merciless. "I began to suspect something queer. Last night I took the one way to make certain— obtained your finger-prints from that pen and that specially prepared sheet of paper. They've just been brought up. Here they are. Identical with those of Kilraine. Fingerprints don't lie."

So the blow fell.

Cabot pressed out his cigarette. He was fighting now, silently, invisibly, his brain reaching out, his whole self trying to grapple with this man mentally. But the shock was numbing. When he needed them most, his amazing mental powers failed him.

In a flash, he saw what this meant. Utter ruin. He was identified with Kilraine, and confirmation could be obtained in a dozen quarters.

"Nobody else knows this, Cabot," said Winthrop Blake suddenly.

Cabot ignored the words, their implication. He leaned forward, earnestly.

"It's true, Blake," he said. "As Kilraine, I've done no wrong; indeed, I've done much for society. Kilraine turned in the kidnapers of the Carson child, and other crooks. Thanks to

Kilraine, the Wurzle gang was wiped out. Kilraine didn't kill Ben Carias, but it was thought he did—"

His words died away under the unsmiling fixed regard of Winthrop Blake. At last his brain caught a warning, a horrible warning that shocked him again. Then Blake spoke.

"Fifty thousand dollars, Cabot, and I'll destroy this paper!"

Cabot stared. "What? Blake, do you know what you're saying?"

"Naturally. You're caught. Pay up."

Blackmail, then! This man, of all others!

"So!" murmured Cabot. "You're glad he doesn't know about it, are you?"

Winthrop Blake started. His eyes dilated slightly.

"Eh? What do you mean?"

"You know what I mean. What's his name, Blake? The Big Shot!"

"You'd better sing low and sing soft, Cabot," said the other. "Let me tell you, the Big Shot is the most powerful man in this city, in this state—"

The box on his desk buzzed. He responded, listened, then spoke.

"Send him in," looking up at Cabot, he went on. "I'll get rid of this fellow while you think over the matter—and think hard. You're caught, remember."

The door opened. Into the room shambled a man, well-dressed, but pallid, twitchy, furtive. Cabot recognized him as an acquaintance of Kilraine, one Hoppy Sam Rolls, a well-known underworld character and supposedly a stool.

"Speak up. Rolls," said Winthrop Blake curtly. "This gentleman doesn't matter."

"It—it's about my girl, commissioner." Hoppy Sam spoke up, indeed, with so fierce a manner that Cabot stared in amazement. Doped up to the hilt! "You framed her, damn you! I just found out about it. You sent her up the river! Now, you write out an order to release her, see? Do it quick, damn you!"

Blake broke into a laugh. "Hello, Sam! Feeling good, aren't you? Giving me orders, huh? Clear out of here, before I have you thrown out."

"Aw, have a heart, commissioner!" Hoppy Sam edged about the desk, held out a pleading hand. "You know she ain't a bad sort. Them bulls framed her and you backed 'em up—"

"Get out!" snapped Blake and reached into an open drawer.

Like a flash, moving so quickly that the eye could scarcely follow him, the dope addict leaped.

Winthrop Blake came to his feet, jerking up a pistol. Hoppy Sam grappled with him, mouthing insane curses. The pistol roared, then roared a second time. The two men rocked back and forth. From Sam burst a wild and unearthly scream. The office door was flung open, but too late. The locked figures struck the desk, rebounded, reeled at the wide open window, fell across the sill, hung there. From Blake broke one appalling cry.

John Cabot leaped forward—too late! His fingers caught Blake's ankle, but his hold was jerked loose. The intertwined, twisting figures were gone, jerking away into space. A voice wailed up emptily and then was hushed.

Weak and sick, Cabot leaned against the desk. He felt in his pocket, at the pressure of the box there. Then he glanced around. The room was in a turmoil—officers, clerks, under-cover men. It had happened before their very eyes, as they rushed in. No need to ask questions.

For the last time, the fingers of Korvo the Great moved swiftly, invisibly, deftly.

A newspaper man broke in, as Cabot was telling his story, pointing to the box and the emeralds on the desk.

"My God, what a yarn!" he cried out. "Listen here, Mr. Cabot—you say he got this bird with the goods, eh? Recovered these Templehof emeralds? Last thing he did? Holy smoke, what a story! Look at the banner—heroic death of police commissioner—"

Cabot went stumbling out. He was still weak, still rather sick at the horror of it. But, as he left the building and stood waiting on the curb for Bowker to bring up the car, he was tearing a strip of paper across and across, into tiny splinters that lifted and were gone into the street—bearing with them the damning finger-prints.

Only Winthrop Blake had known. And Winthrop Blake would not tell.

THE MAN WITH THE RUBBER FACE

FACING RUIN, DISGRACE—DEATH, JOHN CABOT, WHO
COULD CHANGE HIS IDENTITY AT WILL, WAGED SINGLE-
HANDED WAR ON THE CZAR OF CRIME—THE MYSTERIOUS,
UNKNOWN RULER OF THE UNDERWORLD!

S CARCELY HAD John Cabot settled into his desk
chair, when the door of the outer office was flung open.
Mary Sargent, the manager of the Cabot Estate, hurriedly came
forward and slapped down a morning paper.

"Good morning—have you read about it?" she demanded.

Cabot smiled. He had rarely seen her so flushed with excite-
ment.

"Haven't glanced at the paper yet, Mary—"

"Then read this!" She shoved the newspaper at him, indicat-
ing a front-page banner. "It happened last night. In that model
tenement the Estate built last year. At the very entrance. Two
children! Why, it—it's horrible!"

Cabot scanned the story. His bronzed, whimsical features lost
their smile, drew into hard lines.

Children playing in the street. A car suddenly rushing past, a
hail of bullets streaming at a lounging figure. That of 'Morgue'
Donnor, city bad man. Bullets that missed their mark but struck
down two children instead.

IT'S AWFUL, John!" exclaimed Mary Sargent. "I know
those two little girls. I was there last week, inspecting the building!"

Cabot nodded. A fortnight earlier, Mary Sargent could have
gone direct to the police commissioner, her uncle, with this
blazing indignation. But now Winthrop Blake was dead. A
new commissioner had not yet been appointed. And as she

stood here, shaken by anger and bitter futility, she was beautiful. Supremely beautiful, thought Cabot.

"I think I can find the murderers," he said quietly, "if you'll release me from my promise and let me bring Kilraine back to the city."

She started. "That ex-convict? No! Besides, you know he's wanted for various crimes. He'd not come back."

"He would at my request; I know him well." Cabot leaned forward. "He never committed those crimes, Mary. When he got out of prison, he devoted himself to serving society; but not as a stool pigeon. The police never knew that it was he who solved many a mystery for them. He has a wide acquaintance in the underworld. By tomorrow night he can be in town. Within two days, I'll bet, he can get the murderer of those children. Yes or no? It's up to you."

She stared at him for a moment, a slow pallor rising in her cheeks.

"But his own danger—the police want him!"

"He'll risk that. Yes or no?"

"When I think of those little girls—yes!" she exclaimed impulsively. Then she checked herself and turned. A stenographer tapped and entered.

"Mr. Harmer to see you, Mr. Cabot."

"Bring him in."

Harmer entered; the gray-haired, aggressive lawyer who had handled the Cabot Estate before John Cabot returned from presumed wanderings in Africa to assume the inheritance. He greeted Mary Sargent with a quick kiss. Then, as she departed, he turned to Cabot.

"John! You're the first to know," he said, beaming. "Last night an offer was made me. This morning, I've decided to accept. I'm

It happened—silently, without warning. The night was ripped asunder by stabs of fire, roaring shots.

on my way now to receive the appointment to the same office I held a good many years ago."

"What? Not—"

"Police Commissioner."

Cabot wrung his hand. "Congratulations, Harmer! You're the ideal man—look here! You must make an announcement to the papers, of course. Then say that within three days you'll have the murderers of those two children last night. You know about it?"

Harmer nodded. "Yes. But that's impossible. 'Morgue' Donnor won't talk—"

"He will to Kilraine!"

Harmer reached for a chair. He sank into it, regarding Cabot with uneasy scrutiny.

"John, listen to reason! The police want Kilraine; to a certain extent I can cover you there. But every crook in the city is out for Kilraine, also. He's supposed to have murdered Ben Carias, the gunman. From alley thugs to the mysterious Big Shot himself, the man at the top of half the crime in this state, they want Kilraine. I can't let you do this mad thing."

"You can't prevent me. Mary doesn't dream that I'm Kilraine, remember. But you—"

"I know too much." Harmer shook his head. "As Kilraine the magician, you earned a living. As Kilraine, you were framed and sent up. As Kilraine, you were pardoned and got out to find that John Cabot was a rich man. It's too damned dangerous, John! Once identified as Larry Kilraine, you're done for life! Despite all your ability, which I grant is marvelous, you simply can't buck this game and get away with it."

"Kilraine," said Cabot calmly, "is going to turn in the murderer of those kids."

ALONE IN his office, Cabot reached for his private telephone and called a number. A woman's voice answered. A voice he knew well, a voice Kilraine had known for years.

"Miss Viola Le May?" he asked crisply. "This is Mark Lemon—"

"Oh! You're Larry's friend! The one he said would come!" she broke in eagerly. "And where's Larry? Is he well? Can I do anything?"

"Not over the wire," he said in cold reproof. "May I come to your apartment about twelve?"

"Sure! Come any time you like—"

Cabot hung up, with a grimace. He had put Viola Le May out of his life, for he had a shrewd suspicion that she loved Larry Kilraine. She owed Kilraine much, indeed, but not affection.

Toward eleven, Cabot visited the bank on the street level of the building, and then sought his car, carrying a small grip. Under the wheel of the black limousine was the only man beside Harmer whom he trusted, and who knew his secret. This was Bowker, who had come from prison with him; bull-necked, devoted, grimly faithful.

"Bowker, remember 'Morgue' Donnor? What d'you know about him?"

"Nothin' much, sir. He got out of stir before we did. I heard he's in the booze racket. He near got it last night, too. No telling who tried to get him."

"Right. Go to the Stuyvesant House, on Fifteenth Street. Give me ten minutes."

Bowker grimaced at the hotel's name, and nodded assent.

In the big car, Cabot pulled down the shades, opened the bag, and changed from his own garb to the shabby but neat garments of Kilraine, which he had thought never to wear again. The high false heels snapped on. The old felt hat jammed on over his head. A touch of black to darken his eyebrows. That was all.

Then you saw the transformation, as he sat there. The firm young face drew into oldish lines, haggard, strained; the angle of the jaw, of the eyes, seemed to change—did change! The incredible natural ability to manipulate facial muscles, plus all the intensive practice of long months in a prison cell, did the work. The vulpine, morose features of Larry Kilraine grew.

BOWKER SHOWED no astonishment when from the car stepped the tall, hollow-chested figure of Kilraine, but his eyes darted up and down the street. He knew the peril.

Passing swiftly into the cheap hotel, Kilraine went to the stairs and on up. He knew where to seek. On the second floor, he paused before a door, and knocked.

"Who is it?" came the growl. Kilraine gave his name. With an incredulous exclamation, 'Morgue' Donnor opened and stared. A hulking big fellow, heavy-jawed, heavy-eyed. "You! Kilraine, by all that's holy. Slide in here, you fool! Where'd you come from?"

Kilraine closed the door and chuckled. "I got a hangout, 'Morgue.' The dicks—"

"It ain't the dicks, dammit," snarled Donnor. "The word's out for you! If Morosini hears you're around town, then—"

Kilraine laughed and produced cigars.

"I got friends myself, 'Morgue.' I heard you were in bad, and dropped around. You and me were friends in the big house, and I ain't forgot it. If you need money—"

Thawed, Donnor dropped into a chair and chewed on his cigar.

"Damned white, Kilraine!" he grunted. The man was on edge, keyed up to tremendous tension. "You and me both, huh? We got to watch out for Morosini and Little Joe. Here, let me think—"

He broke off, scowling. Little Joe! Kilraine thrilled to the name. Little Joe, the tommy-gun expert from Chicago, suspected of a dozen murders, convicted of none!

"Who is the Big Shot, 'Morgue'?" queried Kilraine. The other started violently.

"How'd you guess I was thinking of him? I dunno who he is. Nobody knows. Not even Morosini. And now the word's out for me, huh? For us both."

"Might be," said Kilraine. "Just who is this Morosini?"

"He's running the Murder Club—that new night club the society folks are nuts over. I tried to make him take my brand of liquor, see? How'd I know he was running the place for the Big Shot? Well, he is."

For the Big Shot! Kilraine thrilled again. Was he on the verge of learning?

"Morosini is the one that's after you," said Donnor suddenly. "When you killed Ben Carias, you killed his best friend, see?"

Kilraine came to his feet. So that was it! He had everything now at his fingers' ends; the scheme flashed through his mind, full-fledged, perilous, fantastic. He left a hundred-dollar bill with 'Morgue' Donnor, and departed, hastily. Once in the limousine, he went whirling away toward Viola Le May's apartment, and down came the blinds.

JOHN CABOT became himself, but only for the moment. To his own clothes he added a very loud necktie, a huge diamond ring, a dab of grease that darkened and slicked back his hair. His hand moved. A hidden drawer leaped out, a mirror appeared at his touch.

His fingers were deft. Cotton wads filled out his cheeks. A half-inch block of rubber, held between the molars, lengthened his chin; the facial muscles did the rest. A derby cocked over his ear, he inspected himself in the mirror: flashy, arrogant, bold-eyed. Then he spoke from one side of his mouth, barely moving his jaw.

"A hard bird, are you? Well, fool her if you can—and you'll fool anybody."

When Viola Le May opened the door, she shook hands and regarded her caller curiously, then plied him with sharp questions about Kilraine. Mark Lemon shook his head.

"Ain't here to talk." His voice was crisp, sharp, hard. "Larry said to give you this and say that the fifty you slipped him, when he blew, was great luck. Great!"

The brunette cabaret singer, beautiful in her own way and

shrewd enough, tore open the envelope he gave her, looked at the money inside, then tossed it to a table.

"Luck? He's had luck? I'm so glad!" she cried eagerly. "Tell me about him!"

"Nope. I gotta go," said Lemon. "He'll write you or blow in some day. Listen! What kind of a bird is this here Morosini?"

Her startled eyes dilated. "Oh! Leave him alone—he hates Larry! It was Morosini who put a price on Larry's head! He's young, and slick, and the worst kind of bad—leave him alone!"

Mark Lemon said good-bye, turned, and walked out abruptly, even impolitely.

A block away, he rejoined Bowker, dismissed him, and presently caught a cruising taxicab. He had everything he wanted; now for the plunge! If he had fooled the woman who loved Kilraine, then he could fool anybody. Confidence grew in him. Little Joe, eh? Then Little Joe had murdered those children.

H E   L E F T   the taxicab at the entrance to the Murder Club— apparently deserted and empty at this hour, a building lavishly decorated. But, as he expected, a waiter answered his ring, and he found that Morosini—as he also expected—lived here. He was kept standing in the hall until Morosini appeared.

Viola had described him well. Sleek, young, veneered with gigolo polish, dangerous.

"Lemon's my name, Mark Lemon," said the caller in his curt way. "I been a friend of a fellow you know, but now I ain't. You and me might talk business."

"Yes?" The dark, smoldering eyes bored into him. "A fellow? Who?"

"Kilraine."

For an instant, a flash of fire leaped in the eyes. Then Morosini turned, beckoned.

Lemon followed jauntily. The entry led to steps, passing down to the dance floor; in the unreal daylight of the place, an enormous guillotine appeared at the farther end with orchestra chairs around it. A figure was kneeling under the knife, awaiting its fall.

"What the hell!" ejaculated Lemon, as they approached.

Morosini gave him a grin.

"It's not real—part of our attractions," and one swarthy hand lifted toward the low mezzanine balcony encircling the hall. "This way."

Morosini circled the guillotine and entered a business-like office behind it. He switched on the lights and dropped into a chair, scrutinizing his visitor narrowly.

"I'm listening," he said curtly.

Lemon tipped back his hat, produced a stogy, chewed it.

*"By tomorrow night, Kilraine can be in town.
It's up to you," said Cabot imploringly.*

"Maybe you know Kilraine's in town?" he asked.

Morosini stiffened slightly.

"Where?"

Lemon grinned. "Where you'll never find him without help. I ain't in your mob. I'm a stranger in this burg, Morosini. From the Coast, see? If I got a record out there, I ain't telling it. You take me on my face or not at all. Now, Kilraine was visiting with your pal 'Morgue' Donnor only a little while ago. Donnor talked to him, see? That's why I come right here—"

He paused. Morosini was leaning forward a little, intent, watchful. Suddenly the telephone rang. Morosini reached out for it.

"Yeah, myself," he said. "What? He was? You're slow telling me. I know it already. You'd better get in quicker reports or you're out of a job."

He hung up, and Lemon nodded. "Verifying my statement," he observed. "You've got some one watching that hotel, huh?"

"Naturally," said Morosini. "Well, get to business. Donnor talked to you huh?"

"Nope. I dunno him. He talked to Kilraine, and Larry to me." Lemon leaned back. "I'm asking you, feller. Me and Kilraine are pals. I come with him from the Coast. Only, he's broke and living on me, and I'm tired of it. Is he worth five grand to you? On the hoof?"

Morosini eyed him. "Know anybody here in town?"

"Not a soul."

Morosini rose and left the room.

Lemon sat where he was, guessing that he might be watched. He understood perfectly that Morosini was wary, and would not be overtly associated with any enterprise. What a smooth, perfect face the fellow had! Instinctively, Lemon tried to counterfeit it; then an exclamation of surprise brought him from his chair. A man was in the doorway behind him. A small man, neatly dressed, with hot eyes and pallid cheeks. A dope addict.

"Lemon? My name's Joe Bronstein. What's this about Kilraine?"

Little Joe! Lemon chewed on his stogy and hooked his thumbs in his vest.

"Is he worth five grand?"

"Yes," said Little Joe simply. "Tell me about it."

"He don't trust a soul but me, won't go out again, and is waiting to pull off a job," said Lemon. "He's got a room in St. John's Hospital, see? And you can't bump him off there. I'm supposed to be a special nurse and masseur taking care of him. The only time he'll take the air, is night. And I can work it."

Little Joe nodded, quite calmly. "What's your scheme?"

"Well, I got several," said Lemon. "Depends on whether you want him put on the spot."

"I'd sooner get hold of him and take him riding," said Little Joe. "Right now, I ain't in circulation much. I'm waiting to blow out of town myself, but this is too good to miss. Let me think a minute."

He lit a cigarette and leaned back. Lemon watched him, relaxed, Little Joe muttering aloud and his brain worked swiftly. "There's the yellow bungalow on the highway; Colville, over in Jersey; at the edge of town. Everything there, the old Buick, too. Just the thing. Better not delay about it either, tonight—"

Lemon leaned forward. "Tell you what," he said. "S'pose I come here, or where you say, about nine tonight. I'll tell Kilraine I'm hiring a car, driving it myself. You be in a car, see? I'll drive over to the side entrance of the hospital, go in and get Kilraine, and fetch him out. We get into the car, and that's all."

"Yeah?" said Little Joe, softly. "And s'pose you're putting me on the spot, huh? How do I know?"

"Send some one in with me if you like," and Lemon shrugged. "I ain't playing no tricks if some guy is holding a rod on me!"

Little Joe nodded. He brought a roll of bills from his pocket and counted out two thousand five hundred; then handed over the money. He spoke rapidly, low-voiced, and Lemon nodded assent.

"Don't come here," said Little Joe, as he rose. "Come to the drug store on the corner down below. We'll pick you up. What do you say? Oke?"

"One thing," said Lemon, nervously. "I don't want to take any chances on Kilraine coming back, see? I want to know—"

Little Joe grinned "You'll know," he said grimly. "Come on."

He escorted Lemon to the entrance and showed him out. Lemon started down the street, turned the corner, came to where Bowker waited with the limousine, and the next moment was roaring away downtown.

BACK IN his own office, after a bite of lunch, Cabot instructed Mary Sargeant to find Harmer and arrange a meeting with him; it was of imperative necessity. Then, alone again, he picked up his telephone and called the Stuyvesant House. He soon had Donnor on the wire.

"Hello, 'Morgue,' this is Kilraine speaking," he said in the magician's rather husky, throaty tones. "I got to blow out of town, see? You were right. It's too hot here for me. But I picked up something maybe you'd like to know. About that rat Bronstein. Little Joe."

"Yeah? Spill it quick," said 'Morgue' Donnor.

"He's clearing out tonight. "There's a place called Colville, somewhere in the Jersey marshes. He has a bungalow there at the edge of town. A yellow bungalow. That's all I know. I thought it might interest you."

"It sure does," said Donnor's voice. "Thanks a lot! I ain't forgetting you, old man, and if I can do you any good, you holler for me, see?"

Cabot leaned back in his chair with a sigh. Kilraine had spoken for the last time. It was over now forever; Kilraine was no more. He looked up as Mary Sargeant entered.

"Mr. Harmer's at the Union League Club and asks you to come over."

Another fifteen minutes saw Cabot, ensconced in a deep leather chair, speaking rapidly and softly to Harmer, who listened anxiously, but with kindling interest.

"I've learned something, too," said Harmer abruptly. "This Little Joe is wanted for several things, but he's one of those thugs who simply can't be found. So he killed those children, eh? Any evidence?"

"No. Not what you'd call legal evidence."

"I'd sooner have him dead than alive, then—"

"Suit yourself," put in Cabot. "Listen, now! At quarter to nine tonight, have the side entrance of St. John's Hospital covered, understand? Not only covered; have it a regular trap! And everything out of sight. These killers aren't fools. Be careful what men you pick for the job, too! We don't want any leaks. When do you become commissioner?"

"I've become," said Harmer with a chuckle. "Depend on me. I'll make full arrangements."

"Don't forget, now; at least two men inside the entrance. I'll walk in with a gun in my back, most likely, and I want to play safe!"

NINE O'CLOCK found Mark Lemon lounging at the entrance to the drug store, at the corner below the Murder Club. That pinnacle of night life was just starting its evening.

Lemon chuckled to himself, at the thought of 'Morgue' Donnor; Little Joe would be in jail, and 'Morgue' would discover it in a day or so, but would none the less be all the firmer a friend to Kilraine. A good stroke, there.

A car slid up to the curb. A stranger got out and approached him. Slim, young, shifty.

"Lemon?" he asked. "All right. Come along. We got to pick up Joe."

"Isn't he with you?"

"Naw; think he'd take chances, not knowing you? Come on. You drive."

Just the one man. Lemon got under the wheel and drove, conscious of the man in the rear seat, directing him. Another like Little Joe, a hophead, a killer. They halted before a poolroom, and the other alighted.

"I'll get him. You sit tight."

Lemon watched him enter the place. After a moment he came out, with Little Joe at his side. The latter came forward to the car and spoke, cordially enough.

"Hello, Lemon. I ain't taking chances, you see. Everything jake?

"You bet," said Lemon. "Hop in."

They did so. Lemon was starting the engine, when a man was erupted from the pool-room entrance. He came leaping across the sidewalk, calling out sharply.

"Joe! Hey, Joe! Hold on—hold on—"

"It's Frank!" Little Joe leaned out. "What's up?"

The other drew up alongside the car, panting. A pistol suddenly leaped out in his hand; he thrust it forward at Mark Lemon.

"Grab that guy, quick!" he cried softly. "It's a phoney—grab him!"

"He's safe," snapped Little Joe. "I got a gun on him my own self. Spill it!"

"Just got word from the commissioner's secretary—you know, Morosini's cousin!" panted the man Frank. "It's all a stall, see? They got about twenty cops planted all around that there hospital. This here Lemon is some dick from out of town. They tried to reach Morosini and couldn't get him, so got hold of me. It's all a trick to get you, Joe, and this here guy—"

"Is that so?" said Little Joe. "Well, hop in! The three of us will take the bird right along, Frank. The quicker I get out of town the better. Hop in!"

Something crashed against Lemon's skull, and he went limp.

I T W A S a long time before he wakened to a dull pain in his head. He was in the rear of the car now. Little Joe's feet on him. The other two men were in front. They were over in Jersey, careening along at high speeds, driving madly, talking by snatches.

Lemon lay with his thoughts in chaos, then cursed Harmer's secretary to himself. He was ruined, and worse; everything would come out, must come out! They were talking about torture; he could not keep to his impersonation in that case.

"Burn this guy good," said Frank. "I'll guarantee to make him talk!"

"You bet," said Little Joe with relish. "Then we'll drive him down the road in that old Buick, huh? Give him what Kilraine ought to get."

Lemon wrenched at his bonds, quite in vain. He was tied fast. The ghastly certainty of his fate grew upon him with every passing instant.

He resolutely shoved it away. If he could get out of this appalling trap, Harmer must know about that secretary; Morosini's cousin, eh? And then there was Morosini himself, Lemon had glimpsed an audacious, incredible feat, once this matter of Little Joe was ended. But now it would not be ended—not, at least, as he had figured. He himself would be ended, and John Cabot and Kilraine with him. And Little Joe never dreamed that in killing Mark Lemon, he would actually be killing Kilraine!

"Hey, this bird's laughing!" exclaimed Little Joe, incredulous. "Off your nut, Lemon?"

"You'd laugh, too, if you knew the joke," returned Lemon. The other kicked him in the face.

"We're almost there, Frank. Slow down. We'll have the joint to ourselves. See them trees on the right? That's the place."

Lemon was presently hauled half up the back seat, out of the way. The car had turned in a drive and halted. The highway was masked by a line of low trees. Not twenty feet away, the drive ended at the bungalow, and passed around it. A small, cheap structure painted yellow. Trees and high hedges bordered the whole lot, closed it in, made this a little world by itself. A world of fantasy, of horror, centered about a bungalow and garage.

"Frank, run the Buick out here in front," ordered Little Joe. "There's a couple cans of gas in her. Pour one out to let it soak in, and leave the other till we're ready to touch her off. Naw, leave the car. We ain't staying here the night. Come on and gimme a hand with this guy."

Frank departed in the direction of the garage. Little Joe and the other man caught hold of Lemon, jerked him out of the car, and lifted him to the porch of the bungalow. When Little Joe had opened up the door and switched on the lights, Lemon was carried inside and dumped in a chair. The room was ugly, sparsely furnished, gaudy with cheap prints on the walls.

Little Joe surveyed his prisoner. Gone was his amiability; narrow-eyed, intent, cruel, he was himself, the killer.

"Talk!" he jerked out. "That new commissioner put you on this job, huh? Where you from?"

"Chicago," said Lemon quietly. He tried to sense what was in the man's brain, and failed. "No use whining about it, Bronstein. If money will tempt you—"

"Money? You damned rat!" snarled the other. "We'll make a lesson of you for all the dicks and stools to take warning from. How'd you know about Kilraine? Is Donnor in on this, too?"

"Sure," answered Lemon. "So is Kilraine, if you're interested in knowing."

A car engine roared, and presently Frank came into the room.

"She's ready," he said. "Seems like a durned good car to burn up, but you're the boss, Joe. Who's doing the driving?"

"You are," said Little Joe. "We'll pick you up soon's we close the place here, then touch a match to her and go on."

Frank looked at Mark Lemon. "What about him? Bump him first?"

"No. Tie him in and leave him enjoy it," and Little Joe

grinned. "You two carry him out. I'll be right along. He's told us all we want to know."

A paralysis of horror had clamped down on Lemon. He understood their devilish purpose clearly; it was not the first time men had been put out of the way in this fashion. He was beyond help, beyond hope. Money would not avail him. When Little Joe went into the back room, he saw Frank wink at the other man.

"Taking a shot, eh?" said Frank. "Feel like one myself. Well, come on!"

They lifted the helpless captive. Outside, an old car showed in the headlight glare of their own automobile. It had been run out, close to the highway; the keen odor of spilled gasoline reeked in the air as they approached it. Lemon was dumped on the drive beside the old car, and the two straightened up, clear out in the glare of light.

"There's Joe coming now," said Frank. "No hurry."

Little Joe approached from the house, whistling jauntily. He halted abruptly.

"Say!" he exclaimed. "What's that car out there, turning in—"

Then it happened—without warning, without mercy, without another spoken word. The night was ripped asunder by stabs of fire, by a roaring crescendo shots. Little Joe coughed and fell forward on his face in a slumped heap. Frank and the other man were whirled around, jerked sideways; they too collapsed, looking like piles of old clothes in the car lights.

Silence, and sudden as the blasting fire. Then a figure ran forward, caught hold of Lemon, heaved him out into the light, and slashed at the cords binding him.

"Who is it?" came a voice from the car, out there at the end of the drive. It was the voice of 'Morgue' Donnor.

"I dunno," was the reply. "Got blood on his face—hey! Stand up, here!"

Lemon staggered to his feet; but he was Lemon no longer. A

cry broke from Donnor, who came stumbling forward at sight of the haggard, strained, blood-stained features.

"You!" he blurted out, catching the reeling figure in his arms. "You! Larry—"

"Shut up, shut up!" gasped Kilraine desperately. "Don't name me, 'Morgue!' Come over here. Listen a minute—"

"Anybody else around here?" demanded Donner, as Kilraine drew him to one side.

"No, just the three of them here. Listen, now!" Kilraine spoke rapidly, explained what had leaped into his mind. Once wakened to life, his brain was racing ahead, fast and far. "You see? Don't let your own mob know a thing about it. Give out the word that Kilraine's dead. Everybody will think I'm the one found in the car—"

"Grand!" Donnor slapped him on the back. "And it was your tip-off that fetched me here; only we never dreamed of finding you. Look here, old timer! I'm not going back to the big lights. Going straight on south to Miami. With Morosini after me, it's too risky here. He's close to the Big Shot. Why not come along with me?"

Kilraine feigned hesitation, then shook his head.

"No. I'll take this other car of theirs and get back to town. I got to see a moll. May meet you later in Miami. Tell me something! Morosini slipped these birds five grand to finish me off. Why? What's he got against me? It can't be just the killing of Ben Carias—"

"I dunno, for a fact," said 'Morgue' Donnor. "Might be the Big Shot is after you. But I've heard it's Morosini, personal. He sure as hell hates your shadow! There's something we don't know, I guess. Here, I got to be going! We'll get to work."

Kilraine stared into the darkness. Something we don't know! The four words leaped out at him, tantalized him, startled him. Something we don't know!

"Well, perhaps Mark Lemon will find out," he muttered.

Donnor and his companions were gone, with a shouted farewell. The body of Frank had been put into the gasoline-soaked Buick. Those of Little Joe and the third man remained where they were.

Kilraine got into the automobile that had brought him there, started the engine, and ran it out to the entrance. He left it with engine running and returned to the Buick.

Two minutes later, a torrent of fire was hurtling into the sky, to draw the police.

IT WAS nearly three o'clock in the morning.

Morosini was counting cash in his office, when the telephone rang. He picked up the receiver to hear the voice of Mark Lemon, crisp, aggressive, blatant.

"Hello, Morosini! Heard what happened tonight?"

"No. Everything all right?"

Lemon laughed harshly.

"Depends on how you look at it. We were out at Little Joe's place, see?"

"Kilraine was along all right, was he?"

"Yeah." With the word, Lemon breathed more freely. Morosini knew nothing about the warning, then. Nobody knew about it. Frank had been the only person to know. " 'Morgue' Donner showed up and opened on us. That was all. I crawled out from under a car to find Kilraine getting away."

A startled oath burst from Morosini. "What? Hey, where's Joe now?"

"Stiff. I finished off Kilraine, see? I'm the only one that got clear, and I've got a hurt head. I'm laying up for a few days. If I drop in, can you give me a job?"

"I sure can, if you don't talk too much over the wire."

"Had to let you know as soon as I could. All right."

Laughing softly to himself, John Cabot hung up momentarily, then called Harmer's number and waited for a moment.

"Interesting news for the commissioner!" he murmured. "He's got his wish about having Little Joe dead rather than alive. But that secretary of his—that leak must be stopped, and stopped quick! Oh, hello, Harmer! This you? John Cabot speaking. Woke you up, did I? Well, listen—"

THE MURDER CLUB

I T WA S very early, not yet nine, when John Cabot and
Harmer left the Police Commissioner's car and ascended
the steps of the Murder Club.

Morosini, the proprietor, met them inside the entrance and
shook hands effusively.

"We're honored to have you among us, Commissioner!" he
exclaimed. "Yes, I have a table ready, the best in the house. Glad
to meet you, Mr. Cabot."

"The ladies will be here in a few minutes," said Harmer.
"We've heard a good deal about your place, Morosini; everyone
has. We might look around a bit, eh?"

Morosini laughed. "I'll show you around myself, Commissioner. The ladies will be taken care of when they arrive, never
fear. Step this way."

They followed him to the floor of the night club—a place
which had created a sensation upon its opening, and was one of
the sights of the city. Morosini's Murder Club was conducted on
rigorous lines, had never been padlocked, and as the Commissioner murmured to John Cabot, was down on the police books
as practically above suspicion.

There was nothing unusual about the dance floor surrounded
by tables, except that a huge scarlet guillotine, with a figure
kneeling under the knife, towered up at the far end, the orchestra grouped around.

"Wax figure, of course," Morosini observed. "And not a good

one, either. Sometimes, gay sports take it into their heads to let the knife drop, and we must replace the figure."

"THEN THE guillotine actually works?" asked Cabot, and Morosini assented, laughing. He indicated the balcony that overhung the floor, completely around, with stairs leading down at numerous points.

"I'll show you what you may or may not want to pass on to the ladies," he said. "Of course, we pull a lot of tricks on the floor; but here's the big attraction. Not many casual visitors want the mezzanine booths, but occasionally a party does. They're mostly for show."

Cabot had been inspecting the man narrowly. Morosini had regular features, slightly swarthy, smooth shaven; a wide-angled jaw like that of Cabot himself, but more thickly muscled. His black hair was heavily greased and slicked back, but his full evening attire was impeccable. Two glorious rose pearls adorned his shirt bosom.

One odd thing Cabot noticed. The man had dead black hair, yet his jaw did not bear the peculiar bluish tinge it should bear, with such hair. Even when closely shaven.

"This mezzanine is cut up into booths," said Morosini, as they reached the balcony. "I have tables here, and originally figured on using them, but found it didn't work. Once in a while a party uses them. As a rule, however, people come up for a look around. It's not much better than a museum. In this booth, for example, is the famous Carson murder—"

He smiled grimly, as he saw the effect upon his clients.

Each of the dozen booths around the balcony was a deep oval recess, finished to look like a stone grotto. Morosini had pulled aside the curtains of the first to hand. At one side of the recess was a table with covers for four. At the other side were the life-size figures of the Carson case—Carson, himself, the prostrate figure of his wife, and that of her lover whom Carson was in the act of killing.

An exclamation broke from Harmer. "Man, this is wonder-

Cabot jerked the wax figure of Schiller to the floor behind the couch and drew the curtain.

ful! Outside of the Musee Grevin, I never saw such work—hideously life-like!"

"Right, Commissioner," said Morosini. "It is pretty good, for a fact. I've got a Frenchman who did the wax figures. Every one a famous murder case. Here in the next booth is the Williamson group; that dame who killed her children, remember?"

Harmer glanced in, and turned away. "I don't think my wife

would care for it," he said. "It's all right for thrill seekers, but these things are too cursed real!"

Morosini smiled. "But I want to show you my double-barreled one, Commissioner," he said, and led the way to another booth. "You remember, perhaps, the Schiller case in Chicago two years ago? That banker who shot his cousin after the opera one evening?"

"Yes," Harmer nodded. "He was hanged for it, too."

"Right, sir." Morosini threw back the curtain and stepped into the recess. "This is really the finest job in the whole show, but it defeated its own object. It's a bit too gruesome. Since a woman had a fainting fit in here, I usually keep this booth closed up. Sometimes I use it myself, however, for my late supper. My nerves are good, you see."

Cabot looked in. Here was the table, as usual. Opposite it was a couch, upon which was extended the figure of the murdered cousin. That of Schiller stood behind, leaning half over, a pistol in his hand. It was remarkably life-like, as were all these images. Opera hat, evening attire—every detail perfect. Schiller, a smooth-shaven man of rather youthful appearance to have been a banker, wore such an expression of realization, of remorse over his crime, that Cabot was startled. Then Morosini turned to a small curtain at the rear of the recess, which concealed a small niche.

"This will speak for itself," he said, and drew the curtain. In the niche showed a portion of Schiller's figure, hanging by a rope, lit by a ghastly greenish light. The face contorted, horrible, made Harmer turn away with a stifled oath of disgust.

"Nauseating!" he said curtly. "However, Morosini, I suppose there are people who seek the horrible, eh?"

"Plenty of them, Commissioner; the business we enjoy testifies to it. Sorry if I hit your nerves. I'll take you gentlemen back to your table. I've saved one a bit away from the orchestra, halfway down the floor."

John Cabot, alone with Harmer at the table, lit a cigarette and smiled faintly.

"Think you'll show your wife the sights, do you?"

"Damn it, I suppose so," and Harmer broke into a short laugh. "Women seem able to stand such things, somehow. They should be along pretty soon. My wife was going to pick up Mary, you know."

"So Mary informed me," said Cabot, and eyed the older man. Harmer was one of two men alive who knew his secret, to whom his past was an open book. The aggressive old lawyer had been like a second father to him, since he had inherited the Cabot Estate. "What's on your mind, Harmer? Surely the Police Commissioner should be able to take a night off!"

Harmer shook his head. "John, things are in a bad jam. The city is filled with dope, and the police are absolutely helpless. Dope! Heroin, coke, marihuana, every kind of the damned stuff! Somebody has flooded the city with it."

"Not far to see," said Cabot. "The Big Shot is the one, of course."

Harmer grunted. "The Big Shot! I've come to doubt the existence of such a person. That any man could be back of the crime and misery in the largest city of the country and yet remain unknown, mysterious, powerful—is past belief!"

"Well, I believe it," said Cabot coolly. "Want me to look up the dope shovers for you?"

Harmer started, leaned over the table, spoke quietly but with compellent force.

"No, you fool! Listen, John. That's one reason I'm here tonight, to have a word with you in private. You must end all this interest of yours in crime, in criminals. If it ever became known that you served time in the big house as Kilraine the magician, you'd be ruined for life! And you can't play with fire without being burned."

"Maybe," said Cabot. "But because I did spend time in the penitentiary, because I was framed and sent up unjustly, because

I know the underworld, because I have certain abilities that no other man has, it's my place to go to work! But you're not thinking of me. You're thinking of Mary Sargent, aren't you?"

Harmer nodded. "The risk, the heartache. Yes. I think she loves you, John. And she must never know that you were Kilraine."

"Stop! Here they come," broke in Cabot, and rose.

Mrs. Harmer, a thin, kindly woman of fifty, and Mary Sargent were being brought to the table. The conversation was ended, for the moment.

Cabot had no further thought for the topic under discussion. Mary Sargent, in her simple chiffon dinner dress and her cloche hat, was unutterably lovely, and in her smile, in her quiet, calmly poised eyes, all the world was drowned out.

"What about this dope ring that the evening papers are screaming?" she asked. "Is it true or just a newspaper story?"

"I'm afraid it's true, my dear," said Harmer, under cover of the orchestra's blare. "We can't get anywhere, nor can the federal men. By the way, John, I'd know just where to look, if Jenkins were alive today! You remember Jenkins, perhaps? He went up for life, about six years ago, and died in prison last Autumn."

"Jenkins?" Cabot shook his head. "I don't recall him."

"He was the greatest dope smuggler and handler we've ever known," said Harmer. "A queer man, not very old but with white hair and a pink, unlined face. Babyface Jenkins, they called him—"

"Oh!" Cabot started slightly. His gaze met that of Harmer in a mute interchange of swift thought. "Yes, I do remember now. He was in the state penitentiary when he died."

He might have added that Babyface Jenkins had been in the same tier of cells with Kilraine. Harmer, however, had quite understood his quick, flashing glance.

CABOT'S THOUGHTS were abruptly diverted. The lights were switched off. A few skulls, depending from the roof,

glimmered with light. Waiters moved about—walking skele-
tons instead of men. The orchestra was swinging into Chopin's
funeral march. About the dim red guillotine moved a sudden
throng of obscure figures. A ray of light darted at it, lit up the
glittering knife. The knife fell; a scream rang out, abruptly
checked. The lights were on again, the orchestra blaring—just
one of Morosini's "tricks."

Cabot, dancing with Mary Sargent, forgot everything else.
He was intoxicated by her beauty, by her closeness, by her flashing eyes. If he lived a thousand years, no other woman would
exist for him. And he could feel the bond between them, could
feel that for her, too, this same attraction existed.

He and Harmer escorted the ladies upstairs. One or two
of the booths sufficed. Others were looking, seeking thrills;
subdued shrieks sounded from the Schiller murder niche. As
the four descended to their table again. Cabot thought anew of
Babyface Jenkins, who died in prison. The smooth, unwrinkled
features, pink and white; the prematurely white hair. And the
Big Shot—the mysterious, unknown person, whom the city's
criminals themselves did not know? The man who pulled the
strings of crime, whom none could reach!

Cabot started suddenly. He leaned forward across the table,
touched the arm of Mary Sargent. His gaze was fastened on a
woman who had come forward in the spotlight, about to sing.
The orchestra began the barbaric threnody of a "blues" number.

"Look at her!" murmured Cabot. "She is Viola Le May.
Kilraine's assistant."

The others turned, Mary Sargent quickly interested. Her
brows lifted, and she glanced at Cabot with a briefly inquiring
word.

"Assistant?"

He nodded and shrugged. His mind flew back across the
years. Kilraine, the magician, had picked this girl from the street,
had made of her a fine, faithful, perhaps unmoral, woman; had
given her a place in life. There had been no sentiment. Yet he now

knew that Viola Le May had loved Kilraine. Statuesque, splendid in her dark beauty, she began to move among the tables, as she sang. Perhaps the gaze of Mary Sargent drew her insensibly.

She came close, looked at them, smiled at them, sang at Cabot, and went on. Viola Le May knew that Kilraine was dead. She never dreamed that Cabot, sitting here, was Kilraine. Only Harmer knew that. And Bowker, Cabot's chauffeur, who had come with him from prison; faithful, reliable Bowker.

Morosini passed across the floor. Cabot caught sight of him, stiffened slightly, followed the trim, erect figure with his eyes. Somewhere, somewhere! He could not place it. Something about the man brought vague suggestion.

"Where did this Morosini come from?" he asked. "A local product?"

"No," said Harmer. "He opened up this place six months or so back; he's from Los Angeles, I understand, but he has no record and apparently is on the level. Well, I must be in bed by eleven! Don't you young folks want to stay, and let us run along home?"

Mary Sargent gave Cabot an inquiring smile. He shook his head and rose.

"No. The manager of the Cabot Estate must be at work early—and so must I. Earlier than you imagine, perhaps. Mary, let's come here another night and dance the dawn in. Eh? Shall we say Saturday night?"

She smiled assent. They moved toward the entrance. Morosini met them, deprecating this early departure. The evening was not well started before midnight, he said. He himself saw them out to Cabot's black limousine, and held open the door for them. An impressive man, Morosini. And Harmer was the Police Commissioner.

But, as Morosini slammed the car door and waved his hand, Cabot sank back on his seat with a startled, suppressed oath. Something in the attitude, in the gesture, plucked at a chord in his memory. He had it now! Incredible as it was, he glimpsed it in a flash—sat there appalled, unbelieving, tumult in his brain.

He saw suddenly why Morosini hated and feared Kilraine—why there was no bluish tinge to that jaw!

For Morosini was Babyface Jenkins, the man who had died in prison.

THE HARMERS deposited at home, Mary Sargent left at her own apartment. Cabot was alone in the car. He caught at the speaking tube.

"Bowker! Go back downtown, back to the Murder Club. Stop somewhere near there, where you can park. You may have to wait a long time for me."

"Right, sir."

Cabot pulled down the car shades, switched on the overhead light. He was going back there tonight, now. But he was not going back as John Cabot. He must verify this on the instant. He was still uncredulous, perplexed, wondering. Impossible as it seemed, he knew nothing was impossible—yet it must be verified.

A mirror leaped into place. A concealed panel swung out. A hidden drawer slid out. He produced clothes, a soft shirt. Swiftly he changed from evening attire into a sack suit, knotted a neck-

"Look at her!" murmured Cabot. "She is
Viola Le May—Kilraine's assistant."

tie, thrust a big diamond pin into place. Pomatum smeared his hair and darkened it. A derby replaced his silk hat. A touch of black altered his eyebrows.

The magician was at work now, the creature of infinite practise; but something more.

A few wads of cotton in mouth and nostrils, a small mouthpiece of rubber on which his molars clamped. His face was changed. The chin was lengthened. His mobile muscles contracted. In the mirror, Mark Lemon inspected himself, spoke from one corner of his mouth.

"You'll do! Viola knows you, don't forgot. She thinks you're Kilraine's friend. But Morosini thinks you're the man who killed Larry Kilraine—the ex-convict from California! And—does Morosini know who the Big Shot is? We'll see. Yes, you'll do."

The car swung to a halt, backed in against the curb. Mark Lemon alighted and went striding jauntily down the street, shoulders back, arms swinging. Not the stride of John Cabot in the least. Bowker would wait there—a week, if necessary.

Ahead, showed the Murder Club. Mark Lemon nodded to the doorman and strode in, and asked for Morosini. He waited by the hat check room.

Across the floor at the upper end, past the guillotine and orchestra, was the private office of Morosini. This was what he wanted to reach. Presently he saw Morosini coming, met him with a cordial greeting, a quick handclasp.

"Well! I'd about given up hope of hearing from you, Lemon!"

"Not me," returned Lemon, crisply. "Say! I dropped in to collect what's coming to me, and have a talk. Maybe it don't suit you now?"

"Sure," said Morosini. "Come along with me."

"Hey! Wait!" Lemon hesitated. "I ain't got the soup and fish—"

Morosini laughed. "Never mind; it doesn't matter. I'm having supper served in a couple of minutes. Better have a bite with me, eh? In a private room. We'll be alone and can talk freely. Come along. I'm glad you showed up. Been looking for you."

He led the way across the floor, and Lemon, removing his derby, followed. To his dismay, however. Morosini did not approach the office. Instead, he turned to one of the stairs going to the mezzanine, and mounted. A moment later Mark Lemon found himself in the booth devoted to the Schiller murder case.

His startled alarm, his uneasiness, was well counterfeited; Morosini laughed heartily, and set him at ease. A waiter appeared. Morosini ordered a double service and settled himself and his guest at the table.

"So you want the balance due you, eh?" he said. "Good. I've got it in my pocket for you now; two and a half grand. Here you are."

Lemon took the envelope handed him, glanced at the bank notes inside, and pocketed it. At this instant the waiter reappeared with a telephone.

"Call for you, Mr. Morosini," he said. "Shall I plug it in here?"

"Yes, and then leave it," answered Morosini. "I may get other calls."

Morosini picked up the receiver in his left hand. His right rested on the base of the telephone.

"Morosini himself," he said. Then, after an instant, his fingernail tapped the telephone base hard—two taps, twice repeated. Idle, meaningless taps. But Mark Lemon started slightly. Two taps, two short dashes! That was the letter M in the Morse code. It would be heard at the other end. A secret signal, proving who was on the line!

"Is that so?" said Morosini. "Yes. I think he's somewhere around now—"

Mark Lemon's brain caught the vibrations pulsing, caught his own name. Question and answer about him. Who was on the line?

"Very well," said Morosini. "I'll give the orders and wait for another call. Right."

*"Damn it, clear out!" Lemon
pulled open the door, shoved
Viola Le May from the room.*

He hung up, sat there for a moment looking down. A thrill rippled through Mark Lemon. The Big Shot! The Big Shot! Morosini was taking instructions from him—about Mark Lemon! What could it mean? The sense of danger, of acute peril, beat at him with imperious insistence. Then Morosini looked up, smiling.

"I WANT to talk to you, Lemon, about a regular job," he said. "The way you finished off Kilraine speaks well enough for you. Didn't you tell me something about California, and something about a record there?"

Lemon nodded coolly. "If you insist, you got to know," he said. "San Quentin. A five-year stretch. I'm on probation now, and got permission to be here, too. Nothing back there to worry about."

True enough. There was a man in San Quentin of this name—but he was in for life. Morosini nodded.

"All right, then. I expect I can use you. Excuse me one minute."

The waiter had appeared, holding a tray, drawing aside the curtains before the booth. Morosini rose and went to him swiftly, spoke under his breath. For an instant, the gaze of the waiter flashed to Mark Lemon, then passed on.

Lemon caught the glance, read it aright. Speaking about him—why? Peril, peril! The sense of it was suffocating, yet he had to sit here, apparently noticing nothing. The waiter came forward, put down his tray. Morosini resumed his seat. Then the waiter departed hurriedly.

Morosini talked on, affably, and Lemon could catch nothing from his brain. But no need. He knew now why Morosini hated Kilraine, a man who had known Babyface Jenkins in the big house and who might threaten this imposture. The white hair dyed black, the swarthy stain. Probably the tell-tale fingerprints removed—yes! Lemon caught sight of the man's fingertips. They were blurred, the skin was glazed, as from old burns. Clever! A facial operation, perhaps, to boot. Jenkins must have gone through hell before becoming Morosini!

A sudden sharply growing tumult. A waiter burst in between the curtains.

"Mr. Morosini! There's a hell of a fight, going on down there—them college boys that were drinking—you'd better get down—"

Morosini leaped up and darted out, with a growling oath. A scream from the floor, a sudden splintering crash of glass, increasing tumult. And Mark Lemon turned abruptly, as the telephone jangled sharply. The call that Morosini was awaiting!

He picked up the instrument, adjusted his voice to the cool, level tones.

"Morosini himself."

"How do I know?" came a dry, rasping voice. "Hurry up, you fool!"

Lemon's fingernail tapped the telephone base sharply. Two taps, twice repeated.

"All right," was the immediate answer. "Get this straight, now! Dutch and Cornaro will be there in a couple of minutes. They'll take care of Lemon. He's tricked you, you fool! The real Mark Lemon is serving a life term in San Quentin. Did you close all exits like I told you?"

"Yes," said Lemon. The Big Shot! And Mark Lemon was in jeopardy, was doomed! Cornaro was a killer, a gunman.

"YOU GOT to take care of that Le May woman," went on the dry, emotionless voice, "and do it now, tonight! She was Kilraine's moll. Lemon was at her apartment the other day. Have her dropped out of sight tonight, and don't delay. Any word from Anthony yet?"

"No," said Lemon, dry-lipped, tense. Viola Le May—doomed, also!

"You'll hear from him any time. He's landed in town with four trunks full, all safe. Got your arrangements made?"

"Yes. Wait a minute!" Lemon's brain raced. The Big Shot! Here was his chance. If he could seize it—"Look here!" he exclaimed. "I'll have to get in touch with you about that! If I can see you—"

He halted. The hideous sense of failure leaped through him, as he heard a sharp intake of breath at the other end. Then a smothered oath, and a click. The Big Shot had taken warning, had hung up on him! Somehow, he had overstepped, overplayed his hand. He had taken a chance and had failed. And now—

Lemon came to his feet. A quick, sharp step outside. The tumult had quieted. Like a flash, Lemon caught up the decanter from the table, darted to the curtained entrance. The curtains were swung aside and Morosini stopped into the room.

The decanter crashed over his head and Morosini toppled forward, without a word.

NAPKINS, HANDKERCHIEFS; the senseless man was bound hand and foot, gagged. Lemon took the pearl studs from his shirt, pocketed them. Took money from his pocket. Seized the limp and bound figure, dragged it across to the curtained niche where hung the ghastly image of the executed Schiller. Shoving the curtain aside, he thrust Morosini into the niche beside the hanging figure. Barely room, but, enough. The curtain fell again.

No time now to think—every instant counted. The waiter might enter, those two killers would come. No chance to make plans. Already Lemon was in action, his hands moving with the rapidity of light. One chance, and only one! Change his clothes and get out of here before they came for him, before he was trapped beyond escape!

The wax figure of Schiller he jerked to the floor behind the couch. From it, hidden there, he swept the coat and vest and the false front of an evening shirt. He donned them rapidly. Lemon's trousers were black; good enough. This outfit would pass him across the floor, at least. The silk hat leaped to his own head.

"In here, gents," came a voice from outside. "Mr. Morosini's in there. The other guy's with him—"

Caught!

From the stiff hand Lemon wrenched the pistol, breaking the waxed fingers. The curtains were swept aside. Lemon stood at the back of the couch, leaning forward, pistol pointing at his victim. Barely in time, he froze. His features were settled into an agonized contortion.

"He's gone!" cried the waiter. "And the other guy, too! Ain't here!"

Beside the waiter, two other men small, young, deadly of eye. Cornaro and Dutch, the killers.

"They ain't far, anyhow," said the waiter. "Prob'ly in Morosini's office. You gents come on downstairs. We got the doors stopped for that guy, anyhow. Maybe Morosini is showing him the other booths. Come on!"

THE CURTAINS fell again. Mark Lemon relaxed, stood in awful irresolution. He had his choice—a swift, hard choice! He could get away as he was, could get out past the watchers to the street. Bowker awaited him. He could be out of here and away; but what about Viola Le May? At all costs, she must be warned. She, who had loved Kilraine, must be served now as never before.

Morosini's office! If he could get there, if he could find the stain that Morosini certainly kept close at hand—ah, what a game to play, if only for an hour!

Lemon dropped the pistol, stepped out of the booth. The balcony was empty. Next instant he was descending the stairs. No longer was his face that of Lemon. It was that of John Cabot, almost. Certainly, those looking for Lemon would never know him. He came down to the floor, crossed past the orchestra and the red guillotine.

There, just beyond, was the door that led to Morosini's office. As he neared it, Cornaro and Dutch came out, swearing lustily, and stopped to confer. They flung a glance at him, a careless glance. He went on past. Next instant he stood in the office, alone.

The door was locked behind him.

"Send Miss Le May here at once!" he said rapidly, at the desk telephone. "If you get any calls for me, I'm in my office. Get hold of her and send her in!"

"Yes, Mr. Morosini," was the response.

He leaped at the desk, tore open the drawers, searched frantically. Everything now was gambled on the correctness of his theory. Pink-faced Morosini must keep that swarthy stain somewhere close at hand! With it, the way was opening clear before him, and without it, he was still in jeopardy. Ah!

The bottom drawer of the desk. He brought out the bottle, the faintly brown-smeared cloth, laid them on the desk. A tap at the door.

"Come in!" he said, then remembered the door was locked. He rose, and again his face was that of Mark Lemon. He opened the door, stood back. Viola Le May entered and then stood staring, incredulous.

"You! Mr. Lemon!" she exclaimed.

"Yeah. No time for talk," said Lemon crisply. He produced the envelope Morosini had given him, the roll of bills he had taken from Morosini's pocket. He thrust them into her hands. "Take that! Now clear out, quick. Take it on the lam, understand? The word's out for you. You and me both! Account of Kilraine. Get to Cuba, the coast, anywhere! And do it now, tonight."

Alarm, suspicion, flitted across her features, and settled into decision.

"All right. Thanks," she said. "What about Kilraine? Is it true that—that he's dead! Tell me! You must know—"

"He's dead," said Mark Lemon, looking her in the eyes. "Yeah. Morosini done it. I'm turning in Morosini tonight. I've got him laid out now. You clear out of here! Quick!"

A flash of unholy joy lighted up her face at this news.

"You're turning him in! Good! Then—"

"Damn it, clear out!" Lemon jerked open the door, fairly shoved her from the room, slammed the door again and locked it.

He darted to the desk, settled himself there. The pearl studs of Morosini went into his shirt-front. A small mirror came from the desk drawer, and a bottle of black stuff. Washable hair dye. Good!

A pounding at the door. He spoke in Morosini's voice, snarling at them to wait. His fingers were flying, moving deftly, unbelievably—the fingers of a magician.

"Open up! This is Cornaro! We got to see you!"

"Wait, blast you! Wait!"

Hair slicked back, blackened. A quick smear of the swarthy skin lotion, a look into the mirror. It was not perfect, but it might pass. His features had settled into the lines of Morosini's face—good enough at a pinch. He reached forward, unscrewed two of the bulbs in the desk lamp, left one only burning, then rose and went to the door. Everything had dropped back into the desk drawer. Nothing to give him away.

"What the hell you want?" He held open the door, glared at the two men outside. They shoved in, Cornaro speaking rapidly.

"Where's that guy Lemon? We come for him—"

" Y E S ! A N D you're damned slow coming!" snarled Morosini. "You should have come half an hour ago! Somebody tipped him off. He tried to get out, and I soaked him myself. They've carried him down to the river. Fine pair, you are! You can take back word that the job's done, and no thanks to you!"

"Oh! If it's done, then everything's jake. You don't need to get all steamed up," said Cornaro, and turned. "Come on, Dutch."

They were gone. Morosini closed the door, leaned against it for a moment; the strain had been terrific. His nerves ached, his face ached. To hold his jaw, his mouth, his eyes, like those of Morosini was impossible for more than a few moments. He had accomplished the impossible in doing it at all—but he had done it.

He had done it, yes! And Viola, warned, was gone to safety, with plenty of money. Nothing now to keep him here. Sooner or later they must find the real Morosini upstairs. Above all, the Big Shot had somehow taken warning. He had slipped up badly there. Now he must look out. At any moment something might happen.

The telephone jangled. He jumped, then turned to it, sat down at the desk.

"Morosini himself." His fingers tapped out the letter M.

"Hello, there? Say, this is Anthony," came a drawling, impudent voice. "Did anybody give you a ring about me?"

"Yes," said Morosini. "All safe, I hear."

"You bet. Where do you want the stuff?"

The stuff! Four trunks of it, the Big Shot had said! And Morosini had been playing the old game of Babyface Jenkins. Dope. Flooding the town with it, unsuspected. It was for this that the Big Shot had arranged his death, had bribed, worked every trick in the calendar!"

"Bring it here," said Morosini deliberately. "How soon can you deliver it?"

"In fifteen minutes," came the response. "All loaded and ready. Sure you want it there, do you?"

"The back entrance. Right into my office, sure."

"All right. You're the doctor."

Anthony rang off. For a moment Morosini sat motionless, then picked up the instrument and called the Police Commissioner's residence. Presently he had Harmer, sleepy but awake, on the wire.

"John Cabot speaking—is your head clear? Then work, and work damned fast, because I'm in a jam! In fifteen minutes, four trunks full of dope will arrive in Morosini's private office. Morosini is really Babyface Jenkins, who didn't die at all. Never mind asking questions! In exactly twenty minutes, you have a flood of cops here, and get some undercover men here first to keep things in hand! And get this. Morosini is tied up and gagged. He's in the Schiller murder booth, in the little recess with the hanging corpse. Understand? Then move like hell!"

HE TURNED to the desk drawers. From them he raked papers, anything that might be of use, that might give information. He stuffed these into his pocket, clapped the Schiller opera hat on his head, and departed.

The men at the entrance eyed him, without recognition. Despite the swarthy features, he looked like John Cabot. Certainly the evening attire was not the garb of Mark Lemon. No one looked after him. No one followed him to the street.

He came to the black limousine and as he put out his hand to the door, a police whistle lifted and shrilled faintly across the night. Harmer's men had arrived.

"Home, Bowker," said John Cabot, and the car rolled away.

THE LADY FROM HELL

JOHN CABOT STARED AT HER—THE MOST BEAUTIFUL
WOMAN HE HAD EVER SEEN—AND THE MOST DANGEROUS!
THE MAN WITH THE RUBBER FACE FIGHTS FOR HIS LIFE
AGAINST THE ALL-POWERFUL QUEEN OF EVIL!

JOHN CABOT regarded his secretary with infinitely cheerful appreciation. Mary Sargent was also manager of the Cabot Estate, a most efficient manager. The tilt of her nose was delicious. The golden glints of her hair were alluring. Her very presence was like a blessing on the room. All in all, she was the most beautiful thing Cabot had ever seen. He said so, and she dropped him a half mocking curtsy.

"No personalities during business hours, John, as long as I'm in your employ!"

"All right. You are fired," he said, and leaned back in his chair. "Now, what about marrying me? At this moment you're out of a job. Poverty stares you in the face. Consider the future! Will you name the day?"

"I'll name the month, at least," she said promptly. "In May, some time."

"And this is March!" said Cabot. "Two months more, when we might be out at Palm Springs enjoying a California honeymoon?"

"Be thankful for small favors," she retorted. "And now, please, I'd like my job back again—"

THE DOOR of the outer office was flung open. On the threshold appeared Cabot's chauffeur, Bowker. His eyes were dilated. He was breathing hard.

"Beg pardon, sir!" He glanced at Mary Sargent. "I got to see you alone, quick! It's the kid, sir. My brother."

Cabot gave Mary Sargent a nod. "Do you mind, Mary? Bowker is inclined to be sensitive about the shortcomings of his relatives—"

She departed, smiling. Instantly the door closed, Cabot's manner changed. He came to his feet.

"What's happened? I thought your brother was doing a year's stretch?"

Bowker nodded miserably. Between these two men existed

whole-hearted trust. Bowker had been in the big house with
Cabot, had left with him, had remained with him. He was one
of two living men who knew that John Cabot was, or had been,
the convict Larry Kilraine. Bowker, utterly devoted, was more
friend than employee.

"Yes, sir. It seems that he got out two days ago—good behav-
ior. I didn't know it. I just now picked him up as I was coming
downtown. He's in the car now. And—and I guess he's done
for," added Bowker, swallowing hard.

Cabot started. "Done for! What d'you mean?"

"Dying," said Bowker with tragic asperity. "I found him in

*Bowker was fastened
against the wall, naked.
The voice of the girl came
to Cabot's ears. "What
was the connection
between Kilraine and
this man Cabot?*

the street, see? He had flopped. A crowd was gathering. I got him into the car and come here—"

"Injured? Shot?"

"Not that I can find. Near Forty-third Street, it was."

"Why the devil didn't you call a doctor? There are a dozen in the building!"

"I did, sir. Doctor Maine. He's down at the car now, I guess—"

"We can trust Maine. Come on!"

CABOT'S HUGE black limousine was parked before the building, its blinds drawn. As Cabot opened the door, Dr. Maine nodded recognition and pointed to the figure outstretched on the back seat, unconscious, limp.

"Hello, Cabot! I've given him a restorative. No use, though. Who is he?"

"My chauffeur's brother. No use, you say?"

"No, it's a matter of minutes. Here, let me outside."

Maine stepped to the curb, took Cabot's arm, while Bowker entered to join his brother.

"Cabot, he's been pumped full of drugs," said the doctor. "Right arm swollen; the puncture's evident. His heart's fluttering like a leaf! Poor devil; some one bungled a mastoid operation on him, years ago. Facial nerve's severed. No more I can do, except call an ambulance and attend to the formalities. I can make it suicide, of course—"

"Make it murder," said Cabot. "Attend to things, like a good chap!"

The doctor departed, Cabot threw one glance around—the busy downtown street, the vortex of figures, of vehicles, the roar of tumultuous sounds—and then re-entered the car where a man lay dying. A young man, rather heavily built, powerful, the waxen pallor of death already in his features. Queerly arresting features. One side of his face down-drawn, the other side normal; the facial nerve on the left side had at one time been severed. His eyes were closed, his breathing was imperceptible.

Bowker turned with an agonized look. Cabot shook his head quietly,

"Take it on the chin, old man. Any idea of the reason? Drugs, Maine said. Ah! Wait—"

Cabot leaned forward, pushing aside the dazed Bowker, his eyes suddenly intent. The unconscious figure had not stirred; but the brain was not unconscious.

The thoughts came to Cabot confusedly, in a chaotic welter. Many a time this faculty had served him crucially. It was not mind reading. It was the ability to catch the pulsating vibrations of thought from another person, and translate them into words or thoughts. The radio brain, he himself called it. Nothing that he could switch on and off at will; sometimes it was there, that was all. And now it was at work.

"The lady from hell!" came the sharp, clear transmission. "The lady from hell! She's killed me—it's him, him! That damned doctor done it! Both of them! The crippled devil, dark, the scar under his left eye—"

That was all. Cabot started. He stared incredulously. Dark, a scar under his left eye—why, that was the Big Shot, the mysterious, unknown person whose fingers, like tentacles, gripped the city's underworld! Cabot's brain had caught descriptions of him ere this—a cripple? A doctor? Here was something different. Too confused.

Cabot leaned forward again, but drew back. The man's eyes opened, rested on Bowker.

"Hello, Bill!" came his voice, faintly. "They got me. Car waiting for me when I left stir, see? Card—card's in my pocket. She wrote it. Tied me up—left me—but I broke out. They got me, Bill. Tried to make me—make me—I got out, damn them! Look out for her—"

His head joggled sideways, and his brain was stilled.

Cabot's hands slid over the relaxed figure. A card from one pocket. A little money. A packet of cigarettes. Nothing else. The dead wrists were frayed, rubbed raw, the nails torn.

"See it through. Maine's coming back now." Cabot shook Bowker into comprehension. "Arrange the details. Have the undertaker's bill sent to me. Then get up to my office."

As Cabot re-entered the building, the ambulance siren was in the street.

ALONE IN his office, he spread out the articles taken from the dead man. The money he pushed aside negligently, then checked himself, staring. Three banknotes, crumpled, dirty, but each a hundred-dollar note! Cabot whistled softly, and took up the card. It was dirty, too, soiled by greasy fingers, but bore brief writing in a woman's angular script. This writing was in French:

"Laissez passer Charles Bowker comme il veut. Mlle. Francine."

"Hm!" muttered Cabot. "Let Charles Bowker pass as he may wish, eh? This was careless of the lady. Perhaps she never meant poor Bowker to go away with it, though. He had been tied up."

He slipped the card into an envelope, sealed it, and summoned a messenger. After addressing the envelope to the police commissioner, he got Harmer on the telephone. Not only was Harmer an intimate, childhood friend, but he had also been the Cabot lawyer until his appointment as commissioner.

"Harmer? John Cabot speaking," he said. "I'm sending you a card by messenger. Please have the finger-prints brought up and if possible identified, and drop everything else for this job. Today sure. Also, see if any of your squads can give any information on the lady's name; try the speak-easy squad. That is to say, the whole damned force! And Harmer! I'm getting a line on the Big Shot for you—Eh? Doesn't exist? You'll change your mind about that. Please rush this for me, will you? Can't explain now."

AS HE hung up. Bowker came in, a little pale, but bull-necked, scowling, recovered from the shock. Cabot motioned him to a chair, showed him the money, told about the card. The messenger arrived and departed again. Cabot lit a cigarette, leaned back comfortably.

"All right, shoot!" he said. "What do you think happened to your brother?"

Bowker was calm enough. "Somebody was waiting for him when he got out, sure. Tried to make him do something, huh? That money—he never had that much, sir! Only what I sent him. Somebody give him that, then tied him up and shot him full of dope. Chuck always was strong as a horse. He bust out, that's all, but the dope finished him."

Cabot nodded. "Know any woman named Francine?"

"No," Bowker mouthed an oath. "But when I find her—"

"Steady! You won't find her. Remember you were in stir yourself. They'll have you spotted. If you try anything, they'll frame you, send you up again. It's not pleasant; I know.

"Now, I want you to do something. Something damned hard, but necessary. Arrange to get me those clothes your brother wore. The ones furnished when he was turned loose. You'd not want to bury him in those prison garments, anyhow. And there's something else. Wait."

Cabot passed into the toilet cabinet across the office. For several minutes he worked before the glass, slicked his hair over his eyes, exercised his peculiar mobility of feature. This natural gift, brought to perfection by long and patient practise while in prison, had now become an art. A terrible art. Its results passed credence.

When Cabot left the cabinet, Bowker started to his feet with one half-choked cry. For the face was that of the dead man; and it was drooping on the left side, immobile! Unbelievable!

IT WAS close to five that afternoon when a finger-print expert from headquarters showed up with Francine's card.

"The commissioner said to tell you, sir," he reported, "that there's nothing against this Francine woman. She runs a small place on Forty-third Street, a boarding house; there's a speakeasy below, perhaps not connected with her. She's rather high class. In the clear."

"And these finger-prints?" Cabot indicated the card.

"Four or five there, sir. We've only identified one, a thumb print. Belongs Strangler Harris, a wrestler who went bad. Twice tried on manslaughter charges, acquitted; did a two-year bit for assault; under suspicion in the Cantrel murder three months ago, but released for lack of evidence."

"Apparently he has a pull, eh?"

"I wish he was the only one, sir! Any return message for the chief?"

"None, except to thank him for me."

The officer departed. Cabot glanced at his watch; just five. Bowker should have been here ten minutes ago. The telephone jingled. He put out his hand to it.

"Well?"

"This is Bowker, sir. I'm sorry I can't take out the car tonight, sir." Bowker's voice was constrained, oddly hesitant. "It's a touch of the flu, sir. So the doctor says. He won't let me get out of bed, Mr. Cabot. I can supply another man to take my place sir, if you like. A good driver?"

"Very well. Have him here with the car in twenty minutes."

"Yes, sir."

Bowker rang off. Cabot sat motionless, thunderstruck, torn by wild surmise.

The doctor! He caught the clue instantly. Flu? That was nonsense. An hour ago, Bowker had been perfectly well. Something had happened. Bowker had telephoned under constraint. Why? And why another driver?

Harmer had warned him that his past could not be downed unless he broke clear away from it. And in his heart he knew Harmer was right about it. Now they were closing in. They could not suspect the truth, but they were probing. The Big Shot, that master mind of crime! Yet Kilraine was supposed to be dead. It was not Cabot they suspected. It was Bowker, known to have been Kilraine's friend.

"I warned him!" muttered Cabot. "But they struck too swiftly. Got him, somehow. They plan to torture him, make him talk.

That was tried once before, and it failed. Now they're making certain. The same crowd? Undoubtedly. Strangler Harris had handled this card. He was one of the gang that did for Bowker's brother. Shall I turn it over to Harmer, let the police attend to this? No, the trump cards are all mine. They'd bungle it. This is my job."

THE DOOR of the outer office opened, slammed. At Cabot's call, a man advanced into the private office; a trim, lithe man in whipcord. Pleasant-faced but alert, wary.

"Mr. Cabot?" he said. "I'm Bill Anderson, replacing your chauffeur for tonight."

Cabot nodded and motioned to a chair. "Yes, all right," he said carelessly. "I'll be through in a few minutes. Sit down, make yourself comfortable. Here are cigarettes."

He pretended to be going through papers. Anderson relaxed, smoked, kept quiet. And Cabot desperately put his brain to work, tried to probe the man. He could register derision; the fellow took him for a fool, readily tricked. The Strangler would laugh when he heard how easy this was. The Strangler! That name echoed in Cabot's brain.

Well, there was a cool century in this job. Better than helping to break down that simpleton, Bowker! Francine would be having her fun before long, now. She's a bad one, that skirt. Get on the wrong side of her, and heaven help you! Some queer things went on upstairs, back of those doors, too. Remember about that marble step; set foot on it, and you're done for, sure. No danger! Well, this was a soft job—

Cabot put aside his papers and rose, confident that he would learn nothing more.

"Almost ready," he said, approaching the toilet cabinet. "I'll have to wash up."

He closed himself in, fell to work. No delay now! He must gamble everything on one throw of the dice—everything! Consequences he damned. And that boy, murdered only this morning! The marble step, eh? No telling what that meant, but about this man Anderson there was no doubt whatever. Test it out on him, then.

The dead man's clothes; they fit him well enough. A sag in the shoulders, hat pulled down. A look in the glass. Yes, even without the drawn face, this certainly was not John Cabot! Then the face drew down into the awful one-sided immobility of a severed facial nerve. Good! Hard to hold that position very long, though.

ANDERSON STIRRED, rose, turned, as Charles Bowker emerged from the cabinet. A gasp burst from him. His face went livid as he stepped backward. His foot caught in his chair, and he pitched headlong to the floor, scrambling wildly, mouthing oaths.

As he came up, in frantic convulsion of haste, Bowker's boot crashed against his jaw. A cruel, merciless blow that stretched him out, quivering. Next instant Bowker was atop of him, twisting back his wrists, binding them with a towel from the cabinet. His ankles were tied likewise. Bowker stepped into the outer office, closed the door between, and sat down at the telephone switchboard. Presently he caught Harmer at home.

"Hello, Commissioner! John Cabot speaking. At the office. A rascal just came in here; he's tied up. I wish you'd send a couple of officers to collect him. He's concerned in a murder case. Hold him tight. You'll hear from me later. Good night!"

He rang off, leaving the perplexed Harmer questioning the empty wires.

Bowker left the building and summoned a passing taxicab. Temporarily his face was no longer drawn on the left side; none the less, no one would have recognized John Cabot. Upon gaining Forty-third Street, he left the taxi, paid off the driver, and walked slowly along toward the house he sought.

It was exactly like its fellows, all brown-stone fronts; a dozen steps leading up to the door, half a dozen down to the area-way. From this area-way came a man, presently another. Bowker crossed to it, came to the iron door, pressed the button. He did not draw down his face; as yet, he did not wish to be recognized. A slit opened, a man peered out at him.

"Card from Francine, if you've got to see it," said Bowker, flourishing the paste-board. No more was needed. He was admitted, and stumbled down a passage that opened into a long barroom. Bowker took a table and ordered a beer. When the waiter brought it, he looked up, jerked his head confidentially.

"Get hold of the Strangler, will you? I got to see him."

"He was here a minute ago. Went upstairs, I guess. He'll be back."

The waiter moved off. Upstairs? No sign of any stairs in the place. The rear wall was, like the others, gaudily decorated. Before it was a huge and handsome leather screen, against which stood a table bearing the time-honored "free lunch." Presently Bowker saw a man appear from behind this screen, pause at the table, then come forward to the bar. At this hour a comfortable crowd was in the place. The movements of any one person would scarcely be observed.

Bowker rose and went to the table by the screen. He lingered there, with one or two others. Suddenly he caught a slight but unmistakable sound; the soft clang of an elevator door closing. Almost at once a bulky figure passed from behind the screen, swaggering forward to the bar. The heavy torso, the massive, brutal features, indicated that this was probably Strangler Harris.

Without hesitation, Bowker turned and walked behind the screen. There in the wall he detected the door, and tried it. The door slid back. An automatic elevator opened, empty. He stepped in. As he did so, a light flashed on overhead and a slouching figure caught and held the door open.

"Where you goin', there?"

Bowker turned, hand to face, and showed the card. His hand lowered. The guard glanced at him and grunted, sighting that downdrawn visage.

"Oh! It's you again, is it? All right. Go ahead."

Bowker closed the door, pressed the topmost button, and the car moved upward.

He thought back swiftly. Three floors above the street—yes! The odds were even that the topmost floor was comparatively little used. That guard below had known nothing of Bowker's death, obviously—

The elevator halted abruptly, jarringly. Bowker reached for the door, but another hand was already jerking it back. Light flooded on him. He looked into the eyes of the lady from hell.

BOWKER STOOD staring blankly. She was lovely, lovely beyond imagination. A slim, slender girl, rose red and snow white, jewels glittering in her black hair but no more radiant than her eyes. Every feature, every line, of the most exquisite beauty. Her gown a glorious evening thing of black lace, concealing yet revealing in the shrewd chastity that only the Rue de la Paix knows.

Yet in upon Bowker's brain swept the prescience of evil. The subtly overwhelming wave leaped from her beauty to warn him, as she stared in wide-eyed amazement. The lady from hell! She looked seventeen. She might be any age. Bowker waited desperately for his cue. Then it came, as her astonishment broke into words.

"Charles! You—you here! I thought—"

She checked herself, but he caught the unuttered conclusion: "I thought you were dead!" Her hand went out to him, a smile played about her lips, sudden ardent fires lighted in her eyes. Magnetism! The pull of her wrenched at him.

"So you have come back!"

"Yes!" Bowker caught her hand. Abruptly her brain was closed to him. The shock of the meeting was past. She was planning, scheming—all the while smiling upon him—enfolding him in her power, mesh upon mesh of her net twining about him. Personality, sex-hypnotism; names did not matter. He saw how men were helpless before her, sodden fools in her hand.

"I had to come!" he babbled. "I've been sick, see? Queer in

my head. Don't know what happened. My brother tried to keep me. I had to come back, back here, back where you were! Don't be angry with me—"

A flash of gratification, of cruel, laughing exultation, filled her eyes and was gone.

"My poor Charles!" Her voice was low, rich, unutterably lovely. "You are tired. Come, I'll take you to my room. You can wait there for me."

"But not him—not him!" cried out Bowker in sudden terror. "Not the doctor!"

"No. Don't be afraid. He's gone away and he'll not be back," she said soothingly, and her arm crept about his shoulders. "Come! You can sleep until I return."

An awful shiver passed through Bowker. Evil! Evil! The touch of her sent thrills of shuddering horror through him. He could feel what she was. This lovely thing, too young to be stamped with her own character in face and body—the lady from hell, indeed!

THE ELEVATOR door clanged behind them. Bowker yielded to her urge, stumbled along beside her. So the doctor was gone, eh? The actor, the Big Shot! He had taken warning when the real Charles Bowker vanished, then. Too crafty, too wary to remain here!

The room that opened before them was amazing, incredible. And all the while, the pull of the girl beside him, the mental force of her, pulsating through him! She led him to a great soft couch, urged him down, knelt beside him. Almost was he overpowered, felt himself slipping, slipping under her hypnotic thrill, felt her lips brush his face, felt madness swirl through him like a bursting wave.

"Sleep!" she said sweetly. "Wait for me, my dear! Au revoir."

Then she was gone. Bowker, adew with sweat, sat up, tried to get a grip on himself. Even he, warned as he was, had barely been able to resist.

He stared around, sick and horrified by what he felt but could not see—evil! Like the stench of a tiger's lair, was this mental effect. He came to his feet, still staring. He could let his face fall into natural lines again, rest his aching muscles.

The room was large, lit by concealed lights; a symphony in the most glorious golden yellow imaginable. Ceiling, the drapes that hid walls and windows, rugs, pillows, the very furniture—everything was of a rich and glowing saffron. Two divans, a few chairs, many pillows; little else in the room except the marble seat. This was a huge carved seat of magnificent yellow onyx, set against one wall and overhung by a canopy of the imperial yellow silk of China. A huge overflowing canopy, the sheen of its yellow brocade glinting. The chair was on a small platform, and in front of it was a wide step, also of yellow onyx.

"The marble step!" Odd that Anderson should have been so frightened of it, for this slab of onyx held nothing unusual. On either side of it, in front of the canopy, stood six-foot dragons of cloisonne, yellow-glinting lamps depending from their claws. All very gorgeous, thought Bowker, in his one swift glance around, but not what he was after.

He recalled entering the room, and swiftly strode to the silken drapes. A moment, and he located the door. Unlocked. He was in the corridor now listening, peering about. A burst of voices came from his left, as though a door had opened and closed. He turned in that direction. His feet made no sound on the thick carpet.

A low, piercing cry burned through him. Bowker's voice! He caught at a door, flung it open, heard sharp laughter. A heavy curtain fronted him. Trembling, he paused. The voice of the girl lifted to him, clear-cut, close by.

"So you don't like it? Well, you're going to get more of it unless you speak up!" No gentleness in this voice now. It was metallic, edged, shrill with venom. "What was the connection between Kilraine and this man Cabot? You knew Kilraine well. Talk!"

"I—I don't know!" This was Bowker's voice, hoarsely defiant. "You she-devil! I tell you—"

A bell jangled sharply. "Wait!" cried the woman in French. Then, "Hello! Yes, this is she—oh! It is you!"

Advancing, the unseen watcher plucked at the curtain, peered through. He had a glimpse of Bowker spread-eagled against the wall, ironed there, naked. Beside him, holding a long branding-iron in the red bed of a charcoal brazier, stood the man he had seen down below, the Strangler. The girl he could not see, but now her voice came sharply to him.

The lady from hell stood laughing lightly, as she watched their agony.

"Impossible! Anderson cannot be in jail—oh, pardon! If you say so, then it is so. But the brother came back here, I assure you! He is here now, in my room, asleep! He was tame, very tame—ah!"

She caught her breath sharply. Her voice changed, became submissive.

"Very well, doctor," she said, and the watcher thrilled to the name. The Big Shot was on the line, had found out about Anderson! "Very well. I'll make sure at once."

Her hand seized the curtain, drew its folds aside. Then she paused, with a command to the Strangler.

"Wait, I'll be back in a moment."

S H E S W E P T out, not seeing the figure enfolded by the heavy curtain, at her very side. The door slammed behind her. Strangler Harris laughed, and produced cigarettes.

"Want a smoke?" he taunted the naked, helpless Bowker. "Well, your hide will be smoking right quick, so you can enjoy this while I inhale. Shout all you like, too! This place is fixed up to take care of all that. Can't hear a sound outside. Here, let's see if I burned you much—"

He sauntered in front of Bowker, across whose powerful breast ran a red weal. He did not see the curtain move behind him. The long handle of the branding iron extended from the glowing pot, as though inviting a grip. As the iron swished through the air. Harris half turned; but too late. The red-hot end struck him squarely above the ear.

"You!" cried out Bowker. "In his pocket—the key—"

Frantic haste now, deft haste, no motion wasted. Bowker was freed, made a dart for his pile of clothes in the corner. He struggled into them haphazard.

"There's a fire-escape," he cried. "At the end of the hall!"

They were out of the room now. Bowker leading the way, half clad. All vain! The air was suddenly filled with strident clangor;

an alarm gong. Bowker plunged for the end window, tore it open, reached out.

One frightful, incoherent cry burst from him. His body curled, twisted in frantic convulsions. His hands were touching the iron platform outside; touching it, unable to get free from it. Both of them, rescuer and rescued, writhing there in vain agonized futility, pierced through and through by the plunging spasm of electric current.

While, behind them, the lady from hell stood laughing lightly as she watched their agony.

"Killed in a prison break!" she sneered, her metallic voice ringing with venom. "Just like poor Antoine, eh? Killed in a prison break, damn you! But you're not killed yet."

Even in his desperate struggle, the words echoed and re-echoed through the brain of John Cabot. In a flash, he realized everything—too late.

IT WAS nearly a year since Antoine Lafarge, doing a twenty-year stretch up the river, had been killed in the course of a prison uprising. And Larry Kilraine, himself in the big house, had known Lafarge well, had heard him tell of his girl Francine—otherwise Fanny Colby. He had been a cell-mate with Lafarge.

John Cabot was thinking of these things as he waited. He was all but paralyzed. That frightful electric current had left him unable to move his features, temporarily. It was impossible for him to assume any other identity than his own, for the moment. He lay bound hand and foot on a yellow divan, with Bowker beside him, senseless and also bound.

Outside the gorgeous yellow room, Francine was giving orders. Her voice came now and again. Other voices sounded, excitedly. Something had happened. Then she appeared in the doorway.

"Bring him in, if you're sure he was alone," she said.

She crossed the floor with swift, lithe steps. Cabot noted that, as she came to the platform holding the yellow onyx seat, she avoided the slab before it, and stepped up from one side. She threw herself into the seat and regarded the man who was led forward between Strangler Harris and another guard—a man cursing, threatening furiously. An undercover man. Even Cabot recognized the type. He fell silent as he met her smouldering gaze.

"So you came here to pry, did you?" she said, and smiled. "Let him go."

The two freed their captive. He stood rubbing his wrists, staring at the smiling face of Francine. She laughed a little and held out her hand.

"You think I am beautiful?" she said purringly. "Then come, sit beside me! Perhaps we may be friends after all, eh?"

The detective, uncertain, strode forward. He took another step, reached out for her fingers. He stood on the step, on the onyx slab. There was a slight hiss from either hand—a jet of vapor from the jaws of the two dragons.

As the unfortunate man fell, the yellow brocade canopy came down around Francine, closed her from sight. To the nostrils of Cabot drifted the faint, pungent odor of—chlorine? Perhaps. Some deadly gas, at all events, spewed forth by the two dragons. The undercover man lay huddled, motionless.

After a moment Strangler Harris and his companion came forward, picked up the limp figure, and carried it away. They were gone. Cabot caught a sound from behind the saffron canopy; the click of a door closing. The canopy slid back. Francine stood there, her eyes glittering at Cabot. Then she came toward the divan, stood looking down, fiercely.

"You are not that man!" she exclaimed. "You are not the brother of this fool—your face is different! You were made up!"

"Thanks," said Cabot, speaking with some difficulty. He smiled. The muscles of his face were relaxing, becoming normal. "Thanks. Francine. Or should I say Fanny Colby?"

She started slightly. Her eyes dilated.

"What do you mean?" she breathed. "That's not my name!"

"Nonsense. Lafarge told me all about you. I was with him the day he was killed. We had the same cell for six months," said Cabot. "Don't you know that I came here tonight as a joke? I was sent to try it out on you."

"Sent! Who sent you? And you say you knew him?" Color flamed in her cheeks. "Who sent you? Quickly!"

"Shall I say—a gentleman who's a cripple?" replied Cabot. "A dark man, with a scar beside his eye? Some one whom you know very well, in fact! He called you up tonight, too."

She took a step backward. Fear, unmistakable fear, flashed in her eyes.

"He sent you! To do this?" and she gestured toward Bowker. "No! No!"

"Don't be a fool," said Cabot. "Here, let me loose; I'm getting stiff. Take Bowker out of here. Switch off the juice, let him go down the fire-escape! Don't you understand? They're waiting below for him, in the street. To bump him off, away from here. So you're Antoine's girl, eh? He certainly talked about you day and night!"

She flew at him with swift abandon, shook him passionately by the shoulders.

"Antoine did? Tell me about him, everything!" The words burst from her in a wild torrent. Here was the one real, genuine thing in this strange creature's life; her love for the dead Lafarge. "What did he say, that last day? Were you in the break with him?"

"Lay off!" snarled Cabot. "Let me loose, you fool! Get rid of this Bowker first. He's no good to us. That's why the Big Shot sent me. I know everything you need to know."

Pallor overspread her face. "The Big Shot! Then—then you know him—"

"Of course I do!" Cabot swore roughly. "Call the Strangler. Get this bird out of here! I tell you they're waiting down below for him, now!

"All right, all right." She rose, went running lithely to the door, jerked it open. At her voice, Harris and the other man entered. She explained breathlessly. Harris did not know who had struck him down, merely took for granted who had done it. No matter now; they were all in confusion. The girl's orders were supreme; they obeyed.

Bowker, groaning, beginning to revive, was loosened and carried out. Then the girl flew to Cabot's side. She slid a knife from her bodice and released him. He sat rubbing his chafed wrists. She hurled eager words, questions about Lafarge, insistent demands. Cabot spoke briefly of Lafarge, but his thoughts were darting at the platform, at the hidden door behind it. Then he caught at his own name as she uttered it.

"And you know all about Cabot? About what we need to have to hook him?"

"Of course." He looked at her. "What do you want to know?"

"This man Cabot; Bowker works for him. A rich young fool who inherited millions! I want to take him for a big thing, understand? But if it's true about Anderson—"

"It's true," he broke in. "The doctor was going to call you. Yes, they grabbed him. But we'll take care of that. Go on, see if they've got rid of Bowker. Hurry up!"

She did not hesitate to obey him promptly. She rose, went to the door, opened it and passed outside. Her voice lifted. That of Strangler Harris answered in assent. Next moment came a crash, an oath, subdued shouts. Then a burst of laughter from Harris.

"He's gone, all right! Holy mackerel, how he slugged me—"

Cabot was darting to the platform. He gained it, slipped around the onyx seat, felt for a hidden door behind it, behind the yellow drapes. A sharp cry from the doorway. The girl was in the room again, running forward, hurling herself at him.

"What are you doing? Here, get away from there—"

He found a door, threw it open, saw a stairway—then she was upon him in swift fury of suspicion, of alarm, clutching at him. Cabot turned, hurled her away. She staggered, caught out her knife, took a backward step.

She was standing on the onyx slab.

Cabot darted through the opening. He glanced back, had one awful glimpse of her face, heard the scream burst from her as the tiny hissing sound pierced to his ears. Then, as she crumpled up, the door slammed and he was gone.

IN HIS own luxurious bedroom, Cabot set down the telephone and turned to Bowker.

"Get the westbound air express tonight," he said curtly. "Go to Los Angeles and stay there. I'm giving you a check for a thousand; I'll send you more as you need it. Too dangerous here for you and me both. They've run down your connection with Kilraine. If you're gone, I'll breathe more freely, old chap."

"But if it's dangerous for me, sir, what about you?" expostulated Bowker.

"I'm all right. Was just talking with Commissioner Harmer; that hell-hole is being raided now. Anderson has confessed about your brother. He was hard hit by the sight of me. Went to pieces. So you needn't remain on that account. Get off!"

"Yes, sir," said Bowker. "Only, you can't get along without me—"

Cabot broke into a smile. "Here's your check. Get going!"

"Yes, sir," said Bowker, took the slip of paper, and went.

Cabot dreamed that night of a contorted, lovely, agonized face touched by the finger of death. Staring at him, watching him, threatening him. Warning him!

THE HIDDEN CITY

IN A DESPERATE, THRILLING ADVENTURE, JOHN CABOT INVADES THE
LAIR OF THE MYSTERIOUS BIG SHOT—AND THE MAN WITH THE
RUBBER FACE ENDS HIS SINGLE-HANDED WAR AGAINST CRIME!

FOUR MONTHS to a day after the reputed killing of
Larry Kilraine, the private line in John Cabot's office rang
insistently. It was nine-thirty in the morning. Cabot had just
entered the office. He picked up the instrument and answered.

"Yes? Cabot speaking."

"Good morning," came a man's voice, a strange voice. "Is this
the Mr. Cabot who was a friend of Mr. Kilraine?"

Cabot felt an icy hand touch his spine.

"You must have the wrong party," he said quietly, and rang off.

He sat motionless, staring before him. Was it a trap? Only one
person alive had known that Kilraine could be reached through
this telephone number, through him! And Viola Le May had
dropped out of sight months ago. Had she talked? No, she was
true blue. Yet some one now suspected or knew of a connection
between Cabot and Kilraine. A trap, then!

That afternoon, the call was repeated. The same voice. Cabot
answered irritably that he had never heard of Kilraine, and
hung up.

Upon the following morning, Judson Harmer was seated in
the private office when the telephone rang again. Cabot moved
as though to answer, then relaxed in his chair.

"Some one trying to get hold of Kilraine," he said, looking
at Harmer.

Before becoming Police Commissioner, Harmer had been
the lawyer for the Cabot estate. An intimate friend, he was the

only person in the city who knew the full past history of John Cabot, who knew that Cabot had been Larry Kilraine, magician, jailbird, alleged murderer. Harmer listened in frowning silence to the story of the repeated call.

"How many people know your private number?" he demanded.

Cabot shrugged. "Plenty. But only Viola Le May knew that Kilraine could be reached here."

The telephone rang once more. This time Cabot put his hand to it and responded. Sudden pallor leaped in his face. A man's voice. A voice he had heard once, months ago, unforgettably.

Only one person alive knew that Kilraine could be reached through this telephone number. Had Cabot stumbled into a trap?

"Mr. Cabot? I want to ask about a Mr. Kilraine—"

"Go to the devil," said Cabot, and laid down the instrument. Sweat started on his brow. Then, meeting the inquiring gaze of Harmer, a wry smile touched his lips.

"It's happened,"

he said quietly. "The Big Shot himself, Harmer. Asking about Kilraine."

SILENCE. HARMER bit at a cigar, his eyes bright and keen. He hesitated for a moment or two.

"Gad!" he exclaimed abruptly. "We'll have to face it, John. How long is it since you nabbed Morosini for me? Since the word went out that Kilraine was bumped off?"

"One day I found Kilraine's clothes in your cabinet," said Mary. "So it wasn't hard to guess who he was."

"Four months ago," Cabot paused. "Damn it! I wish now I'd talked to him. I cut him off. It jarred me, I can tell you."

"Naturally." Harmer lit his cigar, leaned back in his chair. "Look at this like a police case; the bare facts of it. You earned a living as the magician, Kilraine. You were framed, sent to the big house, later pardoned. You got out, to find that John Cabot had inherited the Cabot estate. Everything was covered up. John Cabot came home from years in Africa. I'm the only person in the city who knows the truth.

"As Kilraine, you turned crook after crook in to the police, solved many a crime. Thanks to your ability in changing your appearance, to your faculty of reaching into the brains of other people, you did great work. But you went too far! Kilraine was supposed to be a murderer; the police were after him; the underworld was after him. You killed him! This Le May woman was his friend. You sent her out of town. She knew that through this telephone number, through a man named Cabot, she could get in touch with Kilraine. Did she know any more?"

"No more," said Cabot.

Harmer eyed him grimly. "Wasn't she in love with Kilraine?"

"There had never been any sentiment between us, upon my honor."

"But there was gratitude. You, or rather Kilraine, did everything for that girl! I warned you repeatedly not to make use of the past. It was playing with fire, John! She was the only person to know of any connection between you and Kilraine. But now—others know. The Big Shot—eh?"

Cabot leaned back. "I see what you're driving at. But Viola would never tell; she is absolutely faithful, Harmer. I'd trust her implicitly."

"Then how have they trailed you down? They suspect, at least."

Cabot was silent.

A tap at the door. Mary Sargent, his secretary and the manager of the Cabot estate, stepped into the office and approached the desk. She laid down a blank, sealed envelope.

"A messenger just brought this."

"Thanks." Cabot laid the envelope aside, and looked up at the sunny-haired, level-eyed young woman who had come to mean everything in his life. "Mary, has any one tried to get in touch with Kilraine, through you or the office?"

"No one," she responded. A troubled look came into her eyes. "I thought that man was dead, John."

"He is," said Cabot. "That's all, thanks."

WHEN THE door closed behind her, Harmer leaned forward earnestly.

"John, I'd like to put two of our best undercover men to work on—"

"No," said Cabot flatly, decisively. The old lawyer inspected his clean-cut, bronzed features with a worried frown.

"Damn it! Take my advice, if only for her sake! Stay out of anything involving this Le May woman. You've had enough of it! I wouldn't for the world have Mary learn that you were Larry Kilraine—"

"Neither would I." Cabot lifted his head. "All right, face it! I'm going to probe it myself; certainly there's something queer at work! And if it leads to the Big Shot—then, by heaven, I can do some fighting myself!" Sudden eagerness filled his dark eyes. "Harmer, I'm the only man who has some idea what he looks like, who has heard his voice over the telephone, who has the least line on that mysterious devil! He doesn't trust his own crowd, you know. And with that much of a start—"

"You're a cursed fool!" roared Harmer angrily. "Think you can do what the greatest police force in the world can't do?"

Cabot met those angry eyes.

"Yes," he said quietly. And there it rested.

Only when he was alone in his private office, and had returned to his desk, did John Cabot recollect the sealed envelope left by a messenger. He picked it up and ripped it open. From it he drew a sheet of cheap, ruled paper bearing very fine, copperplate writing—the writing of a skilled, old-fashioned penman.

One glance at the signature, and Cabot leaned back, incredulity in his eyes. As he read the missive, he uttered a low, soft whistle.

"Dear Mr. Cabot:

Being apparently unable to reach you by telephone. I am sending you this. I understand that my old partner Kilraine is dead, and that you would probably know of any papers left by him. He was keeping some for me, and I must have them at once. Will you please have them at your office by five this afternoon? It is of vital importance to me. I'll call for them personally.

Yours truly,
Benny Mullins."

Benny Mullins!

Staring at the writing, Cabot felt the sweat trickle over his temples. Nervous, and small wonder! It was over three years ago, out in Denver; Benny Mullins had died in his very arms. Pneumonia. Benny Mullins, assistant to Korvo the Great—the magician act of Larry Kilraine!

Just afterward, in San Francisco, Kilraine had picked up Viola Le May, had taken her on as his assistant, to replace Benny Mullins.

"This—but this is impossible!" muttered Cabot blankly.

THE PARALYZING fact was that he did have some papers belonging to Benny Mullins. They were in John Cabot's safe deposit box at this moment. The thing was staggering.

What was in that envelope? Kilraine had glanced through its contents, once, long after Mullins' death. He frowned, tried vainly to remember. Something about some crime, a confession; he had not looked into it carefully, for it was of no interest to him. Benny Mullins was far from an angel, though he made a good assistant in the act.

Slowly, Cabot recovered. He knew Mullins was dead; he had buried the poor devil himself. That was fact! Therefore, this letter was a forgery. The man who was coming here at five o'clock was an impostor. Why? To get those papers, of course. Something in them was of value.

"Whoever wrote this," he reflected, "might have known or guessed that I had Kilraine's effects—but he did not know that *I was Kilraine!* That's the big thing, the supremely important thing. My secret is safe! Safe—and yet—"

He shivered a little. Harmer was right. Somewhere, somehow, the toils were closing in. The past would not be denied. One false step, and John Cabot was lost!

Suddenly he caught at the letter, read it again. "Apparently unable to reach you by telephone—" What the devil! It was the Big Shot who had tried to reach him! He knew that voice, metallic, crisp, deadly—a voice that impacted on the brain like a police siren! Then the Big Shot must have sent this letter, must have had it ready to send immediately after his last attempt to reach Cabot, this very morning!

John Cabot went out to luncheon, visited his bank, came back to his office with the brown envelope in his pocket. He had not yet investigated it. Now, alone, he dumped out the papers left by Benny Mullins. He went through them with care.

They were palpably worthless—all but one. Pathetic newspaper clippings wherein Mullins figured as a small town hero. Two love letters. And then the one. A deposition, made out legally in Denver, only a few days before Mullins had died. Pushing the others aside, Cabot settled down to read this carefully.

He frowned over it, startled, astounded. Murder! Murder five years old!

Mullins was explicit about it. Five years ago in St. Louis; the day and date given precisely. The victim, a race-track follower named Hallock, had been shot and robbed of a huge sum. Mullins had aided a Doctor Patrick Pascal in the job; Pascal had planned it, Mullins doing the actual work. Pascal had cleverly thrown the entire blame on a gambler, one Hugo Wire, but in order to blackmail Wire, had kept his evidence secret. Cabot frowned over this, until he comprehended that the canny doctor had so arranged the evidence that it could be used at any future time. Murder is never outlawed.

"What are you blocking the road for?" demanded Cabot. "You!" said one of the gangsters. Pistols had leaped out in their hands.

Seized by his last illness, Mullins repented bitterly. Where Hugo Wire now was, or Doctor Patrick Pascal, he had not the least idea; but he had made out this deposition in a legal manner, his signature being witnessed by a notary public and two witnesses to boot. He also gave full details of the murder of Hallock.

"We don't intend to molest the lady. She can take the car and go; do what she likes. But you're going along with us."

Having digested this singular document, Cabot asked Mary Sargent to get Harmer on the wire. In five minutes he was speaking with the Police Commissioner.

"Hello Harmer! I wanted to ask whether you'd ever heard of a Doctor Patrick Pascal?"

"Not to my knowledge, John."

"Or of any one named Hugo Wire?"

"Wire!" ejaculated the other. "Good Lord, boy! Don't you know who Hugo Wire is?"

Cabot thrilled suddenly. "No! Who is he?"

"Gambler! They say he's back of all the organized gambling in the eastern states! He's usually in Florida or in Atlantic City. No petty crook, but a big business man. Where'd you run into him?"

"I didn't," said Cabot. "Merely his name. Is he in the city? Could he be our man?"

"I hardly think so, John. Of course, anything's possible."

"Well, looks like developments in our case, anyhow. I think I'll change my mind about your offer. I'd like a good undercover man here by four-thirty sharp—that is, if you'll tell him to take orders from me."

"Good! Now you're showing sense!" cried Harmer in delight. "I'll send McArthur over; he's been acting as my bodyguard. Wonderful chap, and he'll be at your disposal. Keep him as long as you like."

"Just for the afternoon, I fancy. Thanks!"

McArthur came; a dour, stolid man with a shrewd eye. He was sitting in the outer office when, promptly at five, Benny Mullins announced himself and was sent in to Cabot.

The latter glanced up, and nodded amiably.

"Mullins? Sit down just a minute; I'm nearly through with this letter."

Mullins took a chair. He was a wary man, thin, seedily attired, with a face like a hatchet. John Cabot went on with the note he was writing:

"My dear Mullins:

Three years ago you were buried in Denver, and your death is duly recorded there. However, I had no use for these papers, so take them.

"John Cabot."

Folding the paper, he slipped it into the brown envelope—in place of the deposition, which now reposed safely in his pocket. Then he swung his chair and looked up.

"Ah, Mullins! You called for those papers, eh? They've been kicking around for some time; ever since Kilraine's death, in fact. Here you are."

He shoved the brown envelope across the desk.

"Thank you, sir," said the pseudo Mullins, looking rather astonished. He took the envelope and hesitated. "Anything to pay, Mr. Cabot?"

"Nonsense, man!" Cabot broke into a laugh. "Run along! Glad you knew where to come for them. By the way, how did you know?"

"Oh! Kilraine said that if anything happened to him, you'd have them," rejoined the man glibly. "You see, him and me used to be partners."

"I see. All right! Good luck to you."

"Thanks. Same to you," said the other, and departed with visible relief.

Cabot lit a cigar, called in Mary Sargent presently, and she gave him a smiling nod as she entered.

"McArthur went out before he left."

"All right, then. Suppose we clean up this matter of tax payments, Mary."

For twenty minutes they discussed the business of the estate, then the private telephone broke in upon them. Cabot seized it, and heard McArthur's voice.

"All set, Mr. Cabot. He ended up at a little house over on Vanderkamp Street—that old-fashioned section. A doctor's house. Doctor Patrick Pascal."

Cabot started. Pascal! The same name! Why, this was monstrous— incredible!

"Where are you now?"

"Down the block from there.

He hasn't come out yet. I'm at a drug store—"

"Then stick around. In half an hour, a man with a gray derby will call on the doctor. He'll come by taxi, leaving it near the drug store. What's Pascal's number?"

McArthur gave it. "Getting dark now, sir. The fellow I trailed here is Hefty Charley. Two stretches for extortion; his lay is the old badger

game. He's a race follower, mostly, and doesn't work the city. Want me to trail him if he leaves?"

"No, he doesn't matter. Follow the gray derby if he comes out."

CABOT LAID aside the telephone. He hastened into the large toilet cabinet near the private door of his inner office. Switching on the light, he fell to work.

*"You talked," acused Pascal. "And you dared to think, you
fool!" As he uttered these words, he struck a match and held
it to the cigar. A spurt of flame came from the corner of the
portrait above the fireplace. The ragged man dropped without
a sound. Cabot was a helpless witness to this tragedy.*

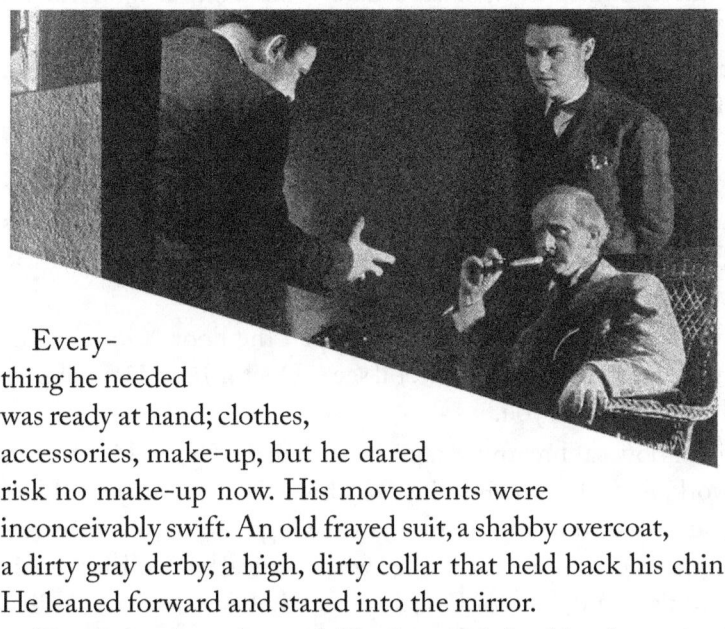

Every-
thing he needed
was ready at hand; clothes,
accessories, make-up, but he dared
risk no make-up now. His movements were
inconceivably swift. An old frayed suit, a shabby overcoat,
a dirty gray derby, a high, dirty collar that held back his chin.
He leaned forward and stared into the mirror.

Slowly, his face changed. The bronzed, healthy features of
John Cabot seemed to melt into those of a stranger!

While in prison, Kilraine had perfected this natural gift.
Months of incessant practise had brought it to incredible
heights. This ability to control his facial muscles, to alter them,
was now a marvelous thing, far past the mere trick skill of a
professional magician. He risked a drop or two of collodion to
keep his eyes pouched, heavy-lidded. Thick-lensed spectacles
concealed this touch of make-up. Necessary, for Pascal now
undoubtedly knew a great deal about John Cabot, personal
appearance included!

For the rest, his muscles did everything; changed the angle of
his jaw, splayed out his nostrils, gave his face a new expression.
And all the while, his brain was probing, wondering. Doctor

Patrick Pascal! The same who had planned that murder five years ago! It was Pascal who had sent the false Mullins, then.

It was nearly dark when the man in the gray derby rang the bell of Dr. Pascal's house. This was a neat brick mansion, set back from the street, in the sedate Vandekamp neighborhood. A house, quiet, austere, lost in the encroachments of commercial structures. The door was opened by an elderly woman in a nurse's uniform.

"Is the doctor here?" panted the caller, pressing one hand against his side. "I got to see him, quick! I got cramps, spasms—something has hit me hard! I can't hardly stand up. My name's Barlow—he doesn't know me. I live at the hotel down the street—"

"Come in." The woman held open the door. "Go into this room on the right and wait. I'll see if Doctor Pascal is at liberty. I think he'll see you."

Barlow sat breathing rapidly. This, naturally, set his heart to work. A flush came into his face, his pulse was quickened. He glanced around the room; plain enough, an office with flat-topped desk, a book-case filled with medical works. Then, to his astonishment, Doctor Pascal appeared. A wheel-chair, pushed by the woman who had opened the door. In it, legs wrapped in a blanket, a thin, frail man of advancing years. Sparse gray hair, gaunt features that were heavily lined and creased, deep eyes, a square, hard chin.

"Come, come!" said Doctor Pascal. His voice was lingering, soft, deeply pitched. It gave the caller a faint feeling of familiarity, nothing else. "I'm a bit of an invalid myself, Mr. Barlow, but still in the ring. My stethoscope, Mrs. Martin!"

He applied the stethoscope, listened; his fingers held the wrist of Barlow. Delicate fingers, but strong as steel. Barlow felt a tingling thrill pass through him at the contact. A man of tremendous personality here, of enormous vitality. The doctor spoke again, questioned, finally relaxed in his chair.

"Prescription pad, Mrs. Martin." His delicate fingers wrote

a prescription. "Here, get this filled. Nothing worse than a gas attack, Barlow. Fee? Nonsense, man! Don't think of it. Get this filled, go home, lie down for an hour. You're all right."

Barlow left the house, walked down to the drug store, hailed a passing taxicab. On the way back to his office, he glanced at the prescription in his hand. Eureka! The same writing—a fine, copperplate hand! It was Doctor Pascal who had written the letter from Mullins—if he needed to know!

Two minutes after Barlow walked into the empty office of the Cabot estate, McArthur shoved open the door and entered. He stared at John Cabot, who was himself again except for the clothes. "My Lord—was it you all the time?" he broke out. "Why, I could ha' swore it was a different man, walked different, looked different! But them clothes—"

Cabot laughed. "It was too dark to see me distinctly, McArthur. Well, that's all, I imagine. I'd like a report on this Doctor Pascal; everything you can learn about him. Say, tomorrow. If I need you again, I'll let the Commissioner know."

McArthur pocketed a banknote and retired, still extremely puzzled.

THE REPORT on Doctor Pascal was complete enough, but not enlightening.

Pascal was a retired physician, with a purely neighborhood practise. He had a reputation for kindness and charity work. He was a paralytic. Of his antecedents, nothing was known; he had occupied this house, which he owned, for about four years.

"I've drawn blank," concluded Cabot, with some dismay. "Certainly the Big Shot telephoned me. Doctor Pascal wrote that letter; Hefty Charley, a known crook, went straight back to Pascal's house. And Pascal, according to the deposition of Mullins, was the worst sort of a scoundrel in St. Louis. Hm! Here, he's a gentle old man, crippled, and whatever we may suspect, we'd never prove anything against him. The Big Shot has probably chosen him for a go-between because of his very infirmity."

And now—what? Lay this information before Harmer! That

*"Take this man to
the Cabot house,"
ordered Pascal.
"Put a bullet into
him and pitch him
out in front of it."*

were folly. The fingers of the Big Shot, as Cabot had learned to his cost, reached everywhere. The police would be slow to get anything definite on Pascal, although they might arrest him for the St. Louis murder. But why remove Pascal! The person to be reached was the Big Shot, the mysterious and unknown super criminal.

"No," determined Cabot. "Now that I've learned this much, I'd better keep the road open to the Big Shot—"

A tap at the door. Mary Sargent entered, her eyes dancing.

"So, John, I've found you out!" she exclaimed blithely. "Your friend at the Ritz has just called up. She wants an appointment with you—she'll either come here or begs you to come there."

"Eh!" exclaimed Cabot blankly. "My friend the Ritz?"

"Yes. She says it's vitally important that see you at once. Do you want to speak with her?"

"Who the devil are you talking about!" demanded Cabot.

Mary Sargent broke into a laugh. "A Mrs. Hugo Wire."

"Good Lord!" Cabot sank back in his chair, Hugo Wire! You're positive? Mrs.?"

"Positive. Shall I put her on the line!"

"No, no! Wait; make an appointment—here, at two o'clock! Let her come here."

Alone again, Cabot stared at the deposition of Benny Mullins, lying before him on the desk. Mrs. Hugo Wire! Why not Wire himself? Why was it that, all of a sudden, ghosts should rise out of the past to assail him? Coincidence?

No. All in one day—Benny Mullins, Pascal, Hugo Wire! Not coincidence. For five years this thing had been lying dormant; the blood of a murdered man awaiting vengeance. For five years the unseen hand of destiny had been slowly shaping events to its purpose, bringing about the proper moment in which to strike.

Hugo Wire! A big gambler, according to Harmer; a well-known man. Why this call from his wife? Why did everyone suddenly know about Benny Mullins' papers? For, undoubtedly, this Mrs. Wire was also after the deposition.

"Something's going on," reflected Cabot. "Something has broken loose somewhere; I'll learn what it is, soon enough. Perhaps from her. Coincidence? Not a bit of it. We'll find destiny at work here. Lucky I didn't send this deposition to Pascal."

PRECISELY AT two o'clock, Mary Sargent announced Mrs. Hugo Wire, and sent her in.

Cabot rose, stood regarding her in the utmost astonishment. She was a young woman, strikingly beautiful, dark, of vigorous intelligence; she was gowned in the height of fashion, in the best of taste. Her sable wrap alone represented a small fortune.

For once, Cabot found himself flung into a species of stupefaction as he bowed her into a chair, murmured polite phrases. This woman, despite the tremendous changes in her appearance, was known intimately to him.

Mrs. Hugo Wire was no other than Viola Le May. Yet, well as she had known Kilraine, she did not recognize him in the man before her.

"Papers? Kilraine's papers? Ah, yes." Cabot came to himself, reached for a cigar to gain time. She had attacked with a furious, breathless vehemence that swept him off his feet, coming straight to the point. Behind her impetuosity, he divined a startling power, a tremendous anger. The woman was fighting, fighting bitterly!

"You *have* his papers, then!" she exclaimed. Cabot nodded. "Listen. Mr. Cabot. Before I married Mr. Wire last month, I knew Larry Kilraine well—had known him for years. My name was Viola Le May."

"He spoke of you frequently," murmured Cabot. "Unfortunately, the owner of the papers came for them only yesterday. A Mr. Benny Mullins."

The woman started. "What? But he's dead! He died years ago—"

Cabot smiled. He was himself again, in command of the situation.

"So I had understood from Kilraine. This man was an

imposter, of course. I did not give him the one vitally important paper; that is here, in my possession."

Her eyes flashed. "The deposition? The confession of Benny Mullins?"

Cabot did not reply. "Come!" he said quietly. "There are some things I want to know. I don't wish to antagonize you, madame. So far as I can tell, that confession belongs in the hands of Hugo Wire—or of the authorities. But before I take any action. I want you to come clean, understand?"

Her gaze, sullen, furious, clashed with his.

"In what way?"

"Every way. First, I understood from Kilraine that he had told not a living soul except you, how to reach him here. Yet, for several days, people have been trying to reach him through me; rather, have been trying to discover if I was the John Cabot

As the man lay senseless, stupefied with the drug, Cabot hurriedly changed into his clothes.

concerned. Unless you betrayed this confidence, how could others learn?"

Silence. The impetuous flame died in her eyes. Presently she nodded.

"Very well," she said in a low voice. "You're on the level. I was Larry Kilraine's assistant in the act, right after Mullins died. One day he showed me those papers left by Mullins. We went through them. I found the confession; then, of course, I didn't know any of the people concerned. I happened to remember that name, Hugo Wire. I advised him to keep the papers, and he did.

"Before Larry died," she went on, "he made me leave town here—for reasons we don't need to go into now. I started for the Coast, but changed my mind and went to Florida. There I met Hugo Wire. Probably you know who he is?"

Cabot assented. "I have discovered, at least, since looking through that confession."

"We were married last month," pursued Viola. "We came to

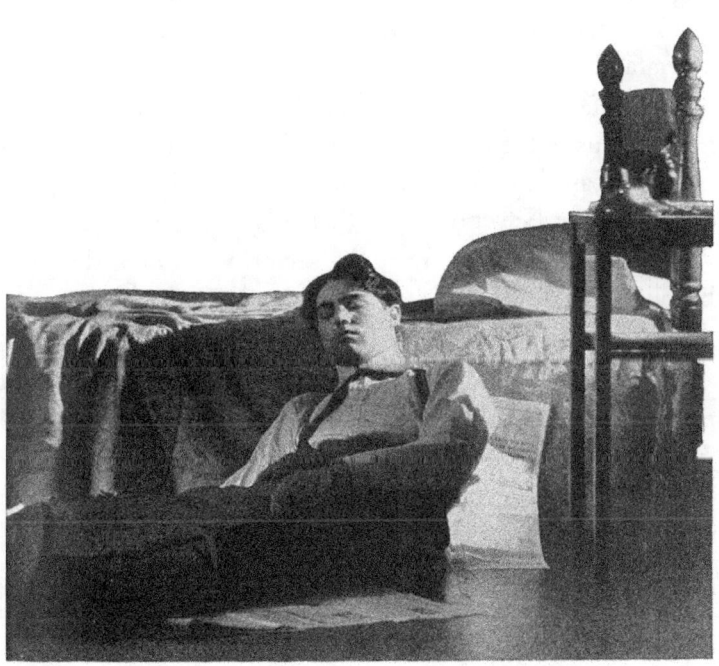

Atlantic City, where he usually lives. He came down ill; influ-
enza, followed by pneumonia. He went to pieces. I had to write
out checks for him to sign. Two of them were to a Doctor Patrick
Pascal. If you've read that deposition, you understand what it
means."

"So!" Cabot whistled softly. "Blackmail?"

"For years past," she answered firmly. "Then I remembered
about the Mullins confession. I had a talk with Hugo. He came
clean with everything. I told him about that confession, told him
that if it still existed, it might be in your hands. He's the finest
man in the world, Mr. Cabot! Now he's down and out, flat on
his back—and I'm fighting for him, understand?"

Cabot met her keen, alert gaze. "Even," he suggested, "if it
means actual danger?"

"Bah!" She made a quick, fierce gesture. "I can take care of
myself. You ask how any one else could have known about you. I
haven't told a soul. I swear it! But, the morning after my talk with
Hugo, we found that the male nurse on the case had vanished.
He must have heard our talk, perhaps had eavesdropped. You
understand?"

Cabot's face cleared. "I understand everything," he said. "Yes,
that explains it. He might have been a spy—undoubtedly was
a spy! He came to Pascal with his story. Pascal tried to get in
touch with me. Never dreamed that—"

Almost had he given away the secret. Viola looked at him
sharply.

"Never dreamed that—*what?*"

"That I knew Benny Mullins to be dead, of course," and Cabot
smiled. "Do you know this Pascal?"

"No. Hugo does. He says the man is something of a mystery.
See here, Mr. Cabot, don't you see that I'm in earnest? I'm in no
mood to stand for much," she went on fiercely. "My husband is
a gambler, or has been, but he's on the level. He's the finest man
I ever knew, and I'll fight this thing through for him until hell
freezes over!"

"Yes, you would," said Cabot. "Kilraine told me you were the most loyal and devoted of women. I gather that there's more to Pascal's blackmailing than merely signing checks?"

"You're a sharp one!" she exclaimed. "Yes. Pascal is trying to force Hugo to give him a foothold in the gambling and race-track business."

"Ah!" This explained Hefty Charley, a race-track follower. The estimable Pascal was branching out, apparently.

"Well, are you going to give me that paper?"

"No."

A flush sprang in her cheeks as she met Cabot's cool regard. Then he went on:

"In the first place, it's not your property. How do I know that your story isn't phoney? And if it were your property, you'd be in danger every minute you had it. I'll put it into an envelope and send it by mail to Hugo Wire, gladly, if you'll give me his address. Then it's safe, and you're safe—and he's safe."

She leaned back in her chair and drew a deep breath.

"Do it, then."

Cabot got out an envelope. Addressing it to Hugo Wire as she dictated, he slipped the deposition inside, stamped and sealed it. He came to his feet.

"We'll go out to the elevator and put it in the chute—"

"Just a minute," she said. "What do I owe you for all this, Mr. Cabot?"

He regarded her with a whimsical smile. "Some day, allow me the honor of telling Hugo Wire how deeply the loyalty of his wife is to be appreciated. Then our account will be squared."

She put out her hand to his. "Thanks, you're a white man! May I use your telephone for a moment before leaving?"

"By all means."

She seized the private line telephone, obtained her number, then spoke rapidly.

"Hello! Mrs. Hugo Wire speaking. Give me Mr. Murchison."

As she waited, she lifted her eyes to Cabot and murmured in explanation:

"Murchison is a lawyer, see? Acts for our friend, the doctor. Go-between."

For the doctor! Cabot started; he guessed the purpose of her call, but it was too late now to check her fiery outburst. She was already pouring out hot words.

"Murchison? Listen! Tell your esteemed client Doctor Pascal that payment is being stopped on the checks sent him yesterday. Tell him that Hugo Wire now has the confession of Mullins and will make use of it. Tell him that in future he can go to hell, and apply it to yourself as well. Good-bye."

She rose, laughing, exultant, and Cabot bowed her out the private door. A moment later the envelope fell into the mail chute, and Cabot shook hands in farewell as the elevator doors clanged open.

Viola Le May had departed out of his life.

AT HIS desk again, Cabot tried to get in touch with the Police Commissioner, to report the interesting things he had learned. He was unable to locate Harmer, but did get McArthur on the wire. The undercover man took Murchison's name to investigate. Then:

"Say, Mr. Cabot! The chief sent me back to look up that doctor, too. This morning. And what d'ye think I found? He's skipped. Yeah! Give up the house and cleared out last night. Nobody knows a thing about him, neither."

Cabot dismissed this with a shrug, and glanced up with a smile as Mary Sargent came into the private office. Beneath his smile, however, was distinct dismay. So Pascal had skipped out! Probably had taken warning from the note put into those papers. Shrewd, eh? And now it was the same old story. A link had been found with the Big Shot, only to vanish at once. Failure once more.

"So!" With a laugh, Mary Sargent seated herself on the corner of the desk and looked down at him. "A surprise, wasn't it? I recognized her at once. Your face was a picture when she walked in! Kilraine's old lady love!"

"Oh! Well, she wasn't that," said Cabot. "You disliked Kilraine—"

"Dislike isn't the word," Mary Sargent said frankly. "And—"

Cabot squared away. "All right, let's have it out, my dear! That woman is fighting for her husband. Kilraine left a legacy behind him, a legacy that will save a man from hell—listen!" And, sketching the whole thing rapidly, he told her of the deposition and its fate.

"The matter is closed," he concluded. "This Doctor Pascal has disappeared, and our last link with Kilraine has been broken. So has our chance of finding the Big Shot."

"I'm glad of that," she retorted quietly. "It isn't your business, anyway, to run down criminals. Oh, I know you think Kilraine had a duty to society and all that! But let the police do the work, John."

"Agreed," said Cabot, meeting her eyes steadily. "This Viola Le May is married. She has gone; we'll not see her again or hear of her. I've done my best in putting the whole thing up to Harmer. My dear, you have my word for it. I'm through."

Her eyes lighted up. "Good! That's what I've wanted you to say, John, what I've been waiting for. And I'm sorry that I spoke of Kilraine's lady love. I only said that to give you a little shock; I didn't mean it to hurt you. Really, I didn't, but…"

Cabot started. Her tone, her look, her words—

"Mary! You can't mean—"

"Yes." She regarded him gravely. "One day I found Kilraine's clothes there in your cabinet; you had left it unlocked. After that, it wasn't hard to guess. I made Harmer tell me the truth, without knowing it."

Cabot felt as though she had given him a blow in the face.

"The truth! That I—that I—"

"That you were Larry Kilraine." She smiled suddenly, put out her hand to him. "Oh, my dear, let's not speak of it, refer to it, ever again! I know enough, I can guess enough; I might even be proud of Larry Kilraine, if I weren't so proud of you! It's ended. Let it stay ended between us!"

"Agreed." Cabot broke into a smile. "It's ended. A new life begins for us both, Mary. You'll not evade any longer?"

"No more evasion, John."

"Then—our marriage—"

"Whenever you say."

For a moment, actions were more eloquent than words. Then Cabot released her.

"Celebration!" he exclaimed exultantly. "We'll leave here at five, skip out to the Windermere Country Club, settle all details—and announce the fact tomorrow! Suit you? And the engagement is going to be a darned short one."

"Suit me? You don't know how much that *does* suit me, John! It's a bargain."

"Then I'll have that chauffeur of mine bring down the roadster and leave it here. I'll have to call the Windermere and order dinner—a special dinner, by Jove! And I'll pick up a bottle of champagne. We'll not have to dress to go out there, either."

SHORTLY AFTER five, Cabot and Mary Sargent left the office. Six o'clock saw the city behind them, and the river; and ahead, the winding country road that led to the Windermere course and grounds.

"Two miles more, and we're there!" exclaimed Cabot, as they swung around a tree-masked curve. "And then—"

Wrr-r-r-ree! Brakes jammed on, tires squealed. The roadster skidded about perilously. Barely in the nick of time, Cabot had sighted the big car lying squarely athwart the road. The roadster came to a halt not a foot from its side. Three men stood looking at one of the tires. They had scattered as the roadster appeared. Now they closed in again.

"What the devil are you blocking the road for?" demanded Cabot, not concealing his annoyance.

"You," said one of the three. Pistols had leaped out in their hands.

Cabot, looking past them, saw that the man sitting under the wheel of the big car was Hefty Charley, the false Mullins.

"A friend of ours wants to see you, Mr. Cabot," said the spokesman of the three. A lean, dark man, entirely at his ease, smiling as he spoke. "If you put up a fight, it'll be just too bad—

Frankie Sylvester, the killer.

for you. We don't intend to molest the lady. She can take your car and go; give the alarm; do what she likes. But you're going with us."

Cabot sat motionless, his brain racing.

Incredible! It was only two or three hours since he had decided to come out here to the club; how had they known, prepared this trap? Well, no matter.

"Who's your friend?" he demanded, struggling to comprehend it, sparring for time. The dark man laughed a little.

"Can't tell you that. I repeat, we have orders to let the lady go."

The very calmness of it all was terrifying. The quiet conviction, the assurance, the lack of bluster, spoke louder than any words. Would they indeed let Mary Sargent go? Then they must be frightfully sure of themselves.

"I see the fake Mr. Mullins over there," said Cabot, more for the benefit of the girl at his side than anything else. "So I take it that your friend is Doctor Pascal."

"That's your guess," returned the other amiably. "Be sensible. Hop out and let the lady drive off. We'll not be caught; there are no strings on her, and she can do as she likes. Yes or no?"

"Looks like yes," answered Cabot. He turned to the white-faced girl beside him and patted her hand. "Cheer up, Mary! Run along with the car and phone Harmer. I'll get in touch with you as soon as I get home."

"All right," she said, fighting back her emotion. Then she took his arm, lifted her face to his. "Good-bye. And good luck—"

An instant Cabot held her in his arms before them all. Then she took his place under the wheel, started the engine, drove off without another word or look, her face intent and desperate.

"Quick, boys!" said the dark man. "She got the number. Switch the plates."

The other two men fell to work applying California license plates over the others of their car. The dark man, beside Cabot, kept his pistol ready. In his left hand he produced heavy handcuffs.

"Hold 'em out."

"Is that necessary?" demanded Cabot. The other nodded.

"Yeah. The boss said to take no chances; this guy Kilraine is a fast one."

Mechanically Cabot extended his wrists, let the handcuffs be snapped home. Kilraine! By the man's face, he saw that his captor was merely repeating something told him.

"Your boss is Doctor Pascal?" he asked quietly.

"Never heard of him," rejoined the other coolly. "And I've never seen the boss, for that matter. Now, Cabot, you sit in front with Hefty Charley. And if you let out a yip as we go along, if you do anything to attract attention, I'll lam you over the head—and lam you hard. Understand?"

At sight of the slungshot, Cabot nodded. He understood. This man had never seen the boss! That explained everything. It was no longer a question of Doctor Pascal.

He was now in the grip of the Big Shot, the man of mystery! And, apparently, the Big Shot knew him for Kilraine.

DARKNESS HAD deepened into night. Back in the city now. No attempt was made to blindfold or gag the prisoner, but Cabot felt the occasional touch of the dark man's hand on his shoulder, knew better than to yield to temptation. It would do him no good at all.

Far uptown, turning aside from the main traffic arteries, they headed for the river. The men behind him spoke, for the first time, as though restraint were now lifted.

"I hear the guy in number one, that calls himself Brown," said one, "is Frankie Sylvester from Chicago."

"Might be," muttered another. "He looks the part. And he's been knocking around the joint for two weeks that I know of."

"You boys got any regard for your health?" asked the dark leader ominously, and the others shut up.

Cabot kept quiet. Frankie Sylvester? Half the country was looking for that gunman, killer, mob leader from Chicago, who had perpetrated the most cold-blooded murders on record. However, at the moment, it meant little to Cabot. His own fate was paramount.

He knew where he was now. They were rolling in under the walls of the old Swabia brewery—a vast brick structure, desolate, abandoned these fifteen years. Not even the change in prohibition had awakened that dead structure to life. Its enormous walls rose empty and dark. The brewery itself had been dismantled years ago.

Dead ahead showed a small garage, built directly against the huge brick wall. The driver honked his horn several times. Iron doors, cleverly painted to imitate the bricks to right and left, opened out and swung back.

The garage opened into another garage—this time within the enormous empty shell of the Swabia brewery!

"Looks like we'd be late for mess," grumbled one of the men, as they alighted.

Cabot, astounded, began dimly to realize the truth. Lights glittered, water splashed across the cement floor. To the right, a dozen cars were neatly racked. To the left, men were at work on other cars, and machinery clanked. A telephone switchboard became visible nearby; the operator before it was a man, who eyed them with lacklustre eyes. Watched them steadily.

Closely guarded, with the dark man in the lead, Cabot found himself shoved through a door and on into another huge chamber, roofless. Here there was less light. He caught glimpses of far-reaching brick walls, of great empty spaces. Close on the left rose a number of frame structures, small bungalows, whose windows gleamed with lights. Men lived here. Cabot caught a woman's voice in shrill laughter, and the sound of it made him shiver involuntarily.

On through another wall, down a corridor, into the open again. Guards armed with rifles halted them, passed them on. And all this in the very heart of a city, unguessed, unsuspected, behind the walls of an empty brewery! The very reality of it was incredible.

Ahead rose their obvious destination; a house-front, with solid brick walls to left and right. More lights gleamed here. The dark man tossed away his cigarette, mounted the steps, pressed a bell. A moment later the door was opened.

And as it opened, Cabot received a terrific blow on the head. Darkness leaped upon him.

HE STRUGGLED through misty ways back to his senses. Voices beat in upon him but failed to reach his brain. Then one voice came, and again, and he wakened to the hot sting of it. That metallic, powerful, vigorous voice he had heard twice before—the voice of the Big Shot!

Then it was gone.

His eyes closed, a splitting pain in his head, he waited. He felt helpless to move. Silence had fallen all around. Gradually, realizing that he was alone. Cabot opened his eyes, verified this fact, and looked about with increasing amazement.

Softly and perfectly lighted by huge crystal chandeliers, the room in which he sat was large, ornate, magnificent. The walls were partially covered by tapestries and by two superb Giordez rugs. A low fireplace, on which burned huge logs, was flanked by massive bookcases, and directly above it, built into the oak paneling, was a portrait, probably contemporary, of Diane de Poitiers. It was a glorious bit of work, a laughing, bawdy, riotous thing, merely head and bust of the ancient beauty. The lower left corner of the portrait was blackened and stained, as though by smoke or fire.

Cabot found himself in a large chair, to which his ankles were fastened. He made no attempt to move, however. The handcuffs on his wrists—what were handcuffs to Korvo the Great, after all? Kilraine had possessed that peculiar ability of the magician, half trick and half practise, of elongating his wrists and hands and slipping them from any handcuffs. This went with his muscular control of feature and body, a part of the old life. For the moment, nothing mattered. He knew escape would be useless. He must be within the building he had last glimpsed— this structure within a structure!

The voice he had heard still lingered with him. The Big Shot in person had been here. Cabot moved his fingers, felt something sticky, glanced down. His fingertips were all black with half-dried ink. Finger-prints! They had taken his prints!

A flat-topped desk, nearby, held a litter of books and papers, a telephone. Beside it was a case of surgical instruments. Beyond, at the end of the room, was a large trestle table, also heaped with books and miscellaneous objects. Then Cabot became aware of a curious thing, but one which he might have expected: there was not a window in this room. It had no need of windows, perhaps, and certainly had no use for any.

A door, opposite the fireplace, was jerked open. Next moment, Cabot saw the chair of Doctor Pascal enter the room; the doctor, himself propelling the wheels, rolled it forward, and the door was closed behind him.

"Well, Mr. Cabot, this is a pleasant surprise!" drawled the deep, musical voice. "I didn't expect to find you here, upon my

*Before Cabot could stop her, Viola Le May
had called a number and was pouring her
fiery message into the mouthpiece.*

word! My dear sir, you have completely shaken my faith in the
limits of human possibility, and in the experience of years."

"How so?" demanded Cabot, rather bewildered. Pascal smiled
malevolently.

"By the way in which you masqueraded as Kilraine. Or did
Kilraine masquerade as you? I should never have believed such
a thing possible! You must be a marvelous make-up artist."

Cabot stared in genuine wonder. Make-up! If this man knew
his secret—did he really ascribe it to make-up? Yet he found the
lined, ascetic features of Pascal quite serious.

"I am rather good at it," he rejoined lamely.

"You were, yes." The penetrating eyes flamed a little. "So you gave that confession to Hugo Wire—or to his wife—did you? That was a mistake on your part. Oh, we all make mistakes! I grant you that. When I sent a man to you, impersonating Mullins, I made a mistake. Good Lord! You must have taken me for a fool. Still, every pup has its eyes opened some day, and mine were opened in time. And how they were opened!"

Doctor Pascal laughed harshly, grimly watching Cabot the while.

"Why did you have me brought here?" demanded Cabot.

"To kill you," said the other, quietly. "In a certain way, for a certain reason."

At this moment the telephone rang sharply. Doctor Pascal swung his chair around to the desk, reached out, and picked up the instrument, but kept his eyes on Cabot.

"Yes?" he said, and Cabot started, eyes dilating on the man. Pascal listened, and then went on. But suddenly Cabot perceived everything—everything! For the voice in which Pascal spoke, was that of the Big Shot!

"VERY WELL. Send him in. Tell Morgan to take his place and wait for the usual signal. No. Let the fool in alone, just as soon as Morgan is ready."

Later, Cabot remembered these words.

At the instant, he was overcome with confusion, with dismay, with baffled anger. This man before him, this cripple, this doctor—the Big Shot! Then his nerves quieted. He suddenly settled himself, realizing that the quiet, deadly answer to his question had been the exact truth. Pascal had fetched him here to kill him, but with a definite reason.

"Your pardon, my friend," and Pascal turned to him, eyes glittering. "You are about to witness something very interesting and instructive. It postpones our little arrangement, but only for a few moments—"

His arms moving rapidly, Pascal propelled himself to the large desk, and swung himself behind it. He picked up a cigar, bit at it, took up a match, then waited. The door had opened, silently. A man staggered into the room, and halted. A ragged, filthy man with wild eyes and gray features, terror in his face.

Cabot knew that tragedy was about to happen before him, but he could not avert it. Nor did he care. His mind was busy now with himself, with his own desperate case. He must fight, as never before, against terrific odds. Yet this man Pascal was human, and made mistakes. He took too much for granted.

"You!" A cry burst from the newcomer, as his haggard eyes fell upon Pascal. "So it is you, after all! As I thought!"

"Yes, it is I," said Pascal, in the voice of the Big Shot. "And you thought right, you fool. You even talked! Don't you know that no man can be right about my identity, and survive? Much less, tell tales! You had a good place here with the others. You weren't content with what I gave you. You had to sneak out to the city. You didn't like the women I provided, eh? You—"

"I didn't mean no hurt, boss!" cried out the man frantically. "It was just to get a moll I used to know, that's all!"

"But you talked," said Pascal. "And you dared to think, you fool!"

As he muttered these words, he struck the match in his hand and held it to the cigar. For an instant even Cabot followed that motion—ah! The old magician's trick that diverts the eyes of the audience! For, from the corner of his eye, Cabot had seen something else—something like a little spurt of flame from above the fireplace where Diane de Poitiers gazed down on the room.

The poor devil by the door had seen nothing. Perhaps he heard the sound of the silenced weapon; but he would neither see nor hear anything again. An invisible hand knocked him down. He lay quiet, a bluish hole in the back of his head.

"You observe," said Doctor Pascal calmly. "Silence is golden, they say; but here, silence is essential."

He paused, drawing enjoyably on his cigar, and smiled.

"I obtained the finger-prints of Kilraine, the ex-convict, vaudeville artist, and murderer, from police headquarters. I have now obtained yours, and as I anticipated, they coincide. In my laboratory, which adjoins this room, I have a large finger-print collection, and I have been busy making an extra set of these duplicate prints. For you."

He drew an envelope from his pocket, tapped it, and tossed it on the floor near Cabot's feet.

"For some time, Mr. Cabot, you sought the Big Shot, as he is inelegantly termed," he went on. "Now you have found him. You know many of his secrets. The police, I might say, are searching the city for you, in vain; they will locate you very shortly."

Cabot understood.

"I mean to have you removed. You will be found with those finger-prints in your pocket," said Pascal calmly. "The police will check up on Kilraine, on John Cabot, as I have done; they will learn everything. You have declared yourself my enemy, and this is my answer to you.

"I am about to put you in the charge of an efficient person, one Sylvester. When you leave this room with him, talk all you like, tell him about me if you like. What matter? Even if he believes you, it is of no consequence. Sylvester will soon be entirely in my confidence, one of the few men who may be completely trusted."

So saying, Doctor Pascal reached out to the telephone.

"Get Sylvester, in Bungalow No. 1," he said. It was the voice of the Big Shot.

Cabot steeled himself. Somewhere, somehow, he must not miss the chance that would come. It would come! It must come!

"Ah, Frankie!" The metallic, vigorous tones again. "I want you to come to my room at once. You will find Doctor Pascal there. You will do exactly as he tells you—exactly! There must be no mistake. Very well."

Cabot comprehended the shrewdness of this man, who with a voice alone, ruled unseen over the invisible empire he had created within four walls.

Now Doctor Pascal, after waiting a brief moment, took up the instrument again. Once more the metallic, piercing voice crackles upon the room.

"Get Dubois!" After a moment: "Ah, Dubois! You did very well with the Cabot errand today. I am about to confide another job to you. A most important one, also. Take one of the Packards and four men—any four you like. Drive down to Atlantic City; leave at once. Hugo Wire and his wife are at the Blenheim Apartments. Get them—both of them! Tomorrow without fail! That is all. Draw five hundred expense money from my secretary."

Pascal hung up, shot a look at Cabot. The latter, however, was still gazing in an abstracted manner at the portrait.

A sharp knock. The door opened to admit Frankie Sylvester. Cabot knew him at once, for the newspapers had been flooded with portraits of him, a peculiar figure, marred by old gang bullets. The left leg dragged as he walked. The right shoulder was higher than the other. Not fat, he was distinctly pot-bellied. His hair was plastered back flat with pomatum. He wore a loud check tweed suit, and held in his hand a cap to match. This was the killer.

"Good evening," said Doctor Pascal in his natural tones. "You see this man in the chair? He is clever, able, desperate; keep your eyes open!"

Sylvester looked at Cabot, and laughed in his throat. The doctor pursued:

"Take that envelope from the floor. Put it in his inside coat pocket. Free his feet from the chair; leave him handcuffed." From an open case on the desk, Pascal took a hypodermic syringe and extended it. "Lead him back to your own room and shoot this into him. It will render him helpless within thirty seconds. Don't leave him until it's finished. Then have him carried out to a car. Go with him. Pick what driver you like and have him take you to the Cabot house; they all know it. Put a bullet into this man and pitch him out in front of the Cabot house. That's all. Do you understand these instructions perfectly?"

"Sure," said Frankie Sylvester. His voice was deep, throaty, coarse. He jammed the cap over his head, took the syringe in his left hand, and advanced to the chair. "A bad guy, is he? Well, he won't be bad long, doc! And I'll be glad of a breath of air, too. All right, guy! On your feet, and start moving!"

"One thing," intervened Pascal. Cabot's feet were freed and he rose. "There must be no mistake, Frankie. Call another guard if you like. If he tries to break away, shoot to kill."

"I guess I can handle him," and a pistol appeared in Sylvester's right hand. "On your way, baby! The doc doesn't want any mess around here, so watch your step and oblige."

Cabot, without protest, advanced toward the door. The pistol was jammed against his spine. As he passed the desk, Doctor Pascal bowed ironically in his chair.

"Good-bye. Mr. Kilraine. A pleasant journey to you."

The corpse of the murdered man still lay beside the door, face up.

The door closed behind them. A hallway led them to the front door; they passed out, and Cabot glanced back to see the strange house-front with its brick walls to left and right. Overhead, the dim depths of the brewery shell, shutting out the night.

Ahead grew a lighted door, the guards chatting before it.

"Orders," growled Frankie Sylvester, as he approached.

"Oke, Frankie," said one, and the guards stepped aside.

This was the corridor; Cabot remembered it, knew he was now retracing his steps. Into the open again, and off to his right showed the little bungalows. Sylvester turned him toward them.

"Head for the first one, guy. Walk right in."

Cabot had tested his handcuffs, furtively. They would work. His wrists and hands, the slim, deft, agile hands of a magician, would slip clear in an instant; but to what avail? Swifter than his hands would be the killer's bullet. Any escape from this place was beyond imagination. And if he died, Hugo Wire would die on the morrow, and Viola.

Escape? No! Fight! Always the audacious, the incredible! The urge drove at Cabot's brain. As they approached the first bungalow—small, one-room affairs—he realized that at all costs he must gain the moment of pause, he must create it! The pause, the diversion, the instant when his illusion could get across. The old stage trick! But no trick would work here. The man beside him would blast out his life.

Cabot halted on the topmost step, turned and regarded Sylvester in the half-light around. The killer prodded him.

"Move on!"

"Wait!" said Cabot weakly. "One minute—it's my heart—"

The other sneered. Cabot exerted himself, opened his brain to the impulses leaping at him from this man; he could sense the vibrations of thought, of ideas. The power was not his to command at all times. Now, when he most needed it, he knew that-ah! Something about Nick the Greek! The killer was thinking about some prior victim. Nick the Greek, the diamond shirt-studs, that night in the Chicago café—

"Move, damn you!"

Cabot obeyed. He had what he wanted; only God knew if it would avail him or not!

THEY ENTERED the one room, whose curtains were drawn.

A bed, a table, a chair. A few magazines, newspapers scattered about, a reading-lamp, a central fixture flooding the room with light. On the table, a telephone. Off one end, past the open closet door, showed a bathroom.

"Set down on the bed. Twist around, your back to me," ordered Sylvester. "We'll get this over with quick."

As he crossed the room to the bed, Cabot worked furtively, desperately. His right hand slid out from the metal ring. Free! He held both wrists together as before, sat down on the edge of the bed, and braced himself. Sylvester paused beside him. Cabot looked up, saw the killer shift the pistol to his left hand, taking the syringe in his right, ready to use. It was the moment.

"You remember that night in the Chicago café?" asked Cabot

quietly. "The diamond shirt-studs, and Nick the Greek across the table—"

Sylvester was inexpressibly startled by the words.

His eyes widened, his heavy jaw fell; for one instant his brain was in a wild turmoil of amazement. The edge of Cabot's hand flickered up across the under side of his pistol wrist. At the sharp impact the fingers relaxed, as fingers must always relax to such a blow. The pistol fell.

Sylvester grabbed for it. A screaming oath burst from him. He fell bodily upon Cabot. But the pistol was gone, slithering somewhere beneath the bed. Cabot's hands were free. He dodged forward and sideways. He gained his feet, the killer frantically clawing at him. The syringe had fallen to the bed.

The two men grappled furiously. Next moment they were on the floor, writhing, striking, thrashing about like madmen, life or death the issue.

Cabot had the thick brown throat under his grip. He lifted, heaved, flung out all his strength. The head flew back, again, again! Each time against the iron leg and foot of the bed. The hoarse oaths died away. The flailing arms fell back. Again! At this impact, the body of the killer relaxed completely and lay quiet.

Panting, his head swimming from his own recent hurt, Cabot rose. He reached out to the syringe on the bed. It was intact, unbroken. He stooped again, bared the man's shoulder, thrust it home. Then he came erect with a shaky laugh. Triumph!

No alarm. The struggle had gone unheard or unobserved. Escape? Ah! That was very different. Yet there was a chance! It was possible. Frankie Sylvester was well-known here. They were all obviously familiar with his singular face and figure and clothes. He was the killer from the West, an underworld hero. Why not?

Cabot went to the dresser, pulled out drawers. Ah! One was heavy. Weapons, a whole collection of them. He reached swiftly for the most deadly of all. An automatic pistol of German make, fitted with a silencer.

Laying the loaded weapon by, Cabot fell to work upon Frankie Sylvester, and carefully stripped the unconscious, hard-breathing man of his garments. They would fit, fairly well. No trouble about that. He removed his own clothes and got into the tweeds, knotted the gaudy silk tie about his throat. No marks of the encounter, fortunately, though there was a distinct bump on his head.

"Take my advice, Cabot. Stay out of anything
involving the Le May woman."

He seated himself before the dresser. The plastic muscles shaped themselves; he reached for the pomatum and plastered back his hair. The lower jaw crept out, the lip protruding. A touch of black on the eyebrows; a burnt match would do it. The nostrils would not do, however. He needed cotton here—ah! There, in the drawer. He rolled it deftly, thrust it into place. Fair enough! Wide, flattened nostrils now.

"His ears are too high; can't manage that," muttered Cabot, inspecting himself. "And I can't get the exact angle of the eyes. Wouldn't pass by daylight, not for a minute, but it's close enough to get over in these lights. Yes, can do! With the walk, all's well."

He went to his own clothes, on the bed, and took out the envelope prepared by Pascal. Two sets of fingerprints. His own, bearing his name, and those of Kilraine from police headquarters. Identical! Pascal had duplicates, perhaps. No matter. Only these would probably bear his name. In any case, Harmer was Police Commissioner and could take care of any others. Cabot struck a match, watched the paper burn up.

He tried the walk. The right shoulder hunched up, the left leg dragging. Chin thrust down—yes, it would pass! What now? He stood reflecting. The necessity for decision spurred him. Then he caught sight of the telephone on the table, and went to it.

A laugh came to his lips as he caught at the instrument. Why not? He might never get out of here alive, and there was an even chance of putting this over. His voice broke upon the silence—but not his own voice. It was the metallic, pulsing voice of the Big Shot, giving the private number of Judson Harmer's residence.

A click; a delay. Then his heart leaped. Harmer was on the line.

"Hello, Commissioner!" Still the Big Shot speaking, rapidly, swiftly. "Pick up five men in a Packard just started for Atlantic City to kill Hugo Wire. John is at the old Swabia brewery, on the river. North Side. You'll need a big force to do anything. The place is inhabited—getting me all right? Hello, Harmer!"

No answer. Silence. A dead line! Sweat started on Cabot's brow. That click, that slight delay! He knew instantly what it must mean. Tapped wires! Probably every line in the place was tapped, watched. The voice of the Big Shot might trick the switchboard man, but would not trick Pascal.

Fool! Fool that he had been! How much, if any, of his message had reached Harmer, he could not tell. And now every instant was precious. He must reach the garage, get out in the guise of Sylvester.

He caught up the silenced pistol, thrust it under his coat, left the bungalow. And as he set foot on the steps, he caught sight of scurrying figures beyond, and heard the voice of the Big Shot—heard it in the air, all around, everywhere. Amplifiers!

"Close all exits! Let no one out! Guards assemble. Investigate Bungalow No. 1 and arrest any unknown person—"

Silence. Like a flash, Cabot turned, went limping across toward the guarded corridor. No escape now! Not a chance to get out. Only the unexpected, the incredible, could give him any hope—audacity! Always audacity!

Instead of seeking an exit, he retraced the way he had come, back to the presence of Doctor Pascal.

Through the corridor. The guards were there, others were coming. "Orders," growled the savage, deep tones of Frankie Sylvester. They knew him, fell back instantly. He went on, dragging his leg, swinging his body, eyes darting around at the shadows.

A moment later he was before the house-front. Two guards coming up at a run. He growled at them. They nodded, flung him a word of recognition. He went on to the door of the house, tried it, opened it, strode inside. Every instant counted now! There was the passage through which he had come. Beyond—

He flung open the door that fronted him.

Pascal was there at the table, alone, talking into the telephone. One glance, then Cabot lifted the pistol in his hand, and fired twice. At the muffled sound of the shots, Pascal turned. His eyes widened.

"Put down the phone! Keep your hands on the table!"

Cabot spoke in his own voice: he could not have hoped to fool this man for long. Into Pascal's face leaped an expression of the utmost amazement. He put the telephone on its rack, left his hands there on the table, staring the while. His lined, square-chinned features became tense. His eyes blazed in comprehension.

"So it's you! Well, well!"

Cabot had already relaxed his taut muscles, let his jaw fall back into normal position. He threw off the cap, then reached behind him and turned the key in the lock of the door. The second door was opposite. He crossed to it, not taking his eyes from Pascal, and shot a huge bolt that appeared. Then he advanced to the crippled man.

In silence he reached out, frisked Pascal, felt beneath the blanket that covered the paralyzed legs. Stepping back, he lowered his weapon.

"But you are a genius!" exclaimed Pascal in a low voice. "You were Sylvester to the life! And it is no makeup. Ah! Now I begin to understand everything!"

"You flatter me," said Cabot drily. The telephone began to ring furiously. "Answer it. Say everything is all right. Call off the alarm."

"And if I do not?" demanded the other.

"It is your life or mine," said Cabot, very steadily. Pascal met his eyes for a moment, read the certainty in them, and picked up the telephone.

"What? Sylvester unconscious? Very well," he said calmly. "Leave him alone and—and end the alarm. The guards to their quarters."

He replaced the instrument, pushed back his sparse gray hair, stared at Cabot. The latter was not standing at the other side of the desk.

"Within the next five minutes, Mr. Cabot, you will be dead. Have you anything to say before it happens?"

Cabot smiled a little. "Only that you are a false prophet, doctor. Oh! What's this?"

Upon the table he saw what he had not previously noted. Neat stacks of bank-notes, clean, crisp, fresh fifty-dollar bills. They bore no signatures. A slow whistle escaped him.

"So this is your secret!" he exclaimed. "Counterfeits, eh?"

"You progress," and Pascal's voice was venomous. Then it changed. "Have I your permission to enjoy a cigar while we talk?"

"Oh, by all means," rejoined Cabot lightly. "You did not finish the one you lighted a little while ago?"

Pascal flashed him a look, but reached out. From an open

humidor he look a cigar, from a tray, picked up a match. He bit at the cigar—and struck the match.

A singular smile touched the lips of Cabot as he looked down at Pascal.

"You forget, my dear doctor, that when I came into this room I fired two shots. And I must draw your attention to a very remarkable thing! Upon my word, I had not dreamed that your portrait of Diane de Poitiers was so extremely life-like! Even to the blood in the veins of the lady—"

A slow, terrible pallor stole across the features of Pascal. As though with an effort, he turned his head and looked up at the portrait.

From the left breast of Diane, where the two bullets of Cabot had pierced the canvas, was running a slow trickle of crimson, down and down across the paneling. In the silence, there was a hiss, then another. Two drops of blood had fallen into the fire.

"I trust," said Cabot, "that your friend Morgan appreciates the instructions in your methods which you were kind enough to give me. I fear he might blame you, however."

The unlit cigar fell from the fingers of Pascal. For a moment his head drooped. Then he lifted his face, gray and terrible. His burning eyes met the gaze of Cabot.

"You have beaten me." His voice was dead, hopeless. "I should have expected it. I am old, crippled, useless. What do you want? What are your terms?"

"Instruct your switchboard operator to put through a call for me."

Pascal obeyed, and handed over the instrument. He wheeled his chair about, came to the end of the desk, and sat there against the paneled wall, immobile, huddled forward. Cabot called Judson Harmer's residence, laying down the heavy German pistol, but not neglecting his victim. A response came.

"Mr. Cabot speaking. Call Mr. Harmer, please—what?"

"He's not here, sir."

"But I was speaking with him only a little while ago!"

Doctor Pascal put out a hand to the oak panel beside his chair, and then leaned his head dejectedly against it.

"Yes, Mr. Cabot, he was here, but he went out very hurriedly—"

The dismayed Cabot, from the corner of his eye, saw the oak panel beside Pascal's chair slide back. He turned, was shocked into inaction. For Pascal was leaping from his chair—the paralytic, on sound and agile legs, was darting into the opening!

Then he was gone.

CABOT DROPPED the telephone, caught up his pistol.

He fired shot after shot, then sprang to the opening. A passage ten feet long showed before him, an electric bulb burning overhead. Cabot hurled himself forward. He came to the end, saw before him narrow stairs descending, and checked himself suddenly.

From somewhere behind was arising a tumultuous din. Confused voices, shouts, a wild uproar punctuated by shots. There was a thunderous hammering at the doors of the room, but Cabot paid no heed. He was staring down at what confronted him, in the light of that overhead bulb.

From those stairs, from the depths below, came the dank smell of water. And there on the stairs, twisted about, staring up at him with unwinking eyes, lay Pascal. That unnatural position, that twisted body, the set features, all told their own story. One at least of those bullets had not missed. Cabot leaned over, saw the dark gouts of blood on the stairs, and then drew back.

He was conscious now of smashing rending sounds. He came to himself, drew a deep breath, turned. One of the doors was being battered down. It burst in. He caught a glimpse of uniforms surging across the threshold. Then the figure of Judson Harmer came striding at him.

"John! All right?"

"Sure. Where's Mary?"

"Safe. I got enough of your message—the word Swabia told me everything! Who's behind all this? Where is he?"

Cabot pointed to the secret passage. "There, waiting for you."

Presently, amid chaos and confusion gradually reducing itself to some semblance of order, the body of Pascal was brought up and carried into the room. A bullet had hit him, yes, but only in the shoulder. The stairs had killed him. His neck was broken.

Suddenly, after excited discussion, Cabot swung around and caught Harmer's arm.

"Look here! Take me out through your lines! I've got an overdue engagement—"

"Forget it, John. You stay right here—this is the most important thing!"

"Not by a damned sight!" said Cabot, with a quick laugh. "Mary and I are being married tonight, do you understand? Married! And not you nor all your cops are going to keep me here, either!"

"I believe you," said Harmer, and clapped him on the back. "Boys, I guess we'll have to let him go—eh?"

The men around grinned and stood back. And in this fashion, John Cabot went to his dinner engagement—and his waiting bride.

ABOUT THE AUTHOR

H. BEDFORD-JONES is a Canadian by birth, but not by profession, having removed to the United States at the age of one year. For over twenty years he has been more or less profitably engaged in writing and traveling. As he has seldom resided in one place longer than a year or so and is a person of retiring habits, he is somewhat a man of mystery; more than once he has suffered from unscrupulous gentlemen who impersonated him—one of whom murdered a wife and was subsequently shot by the police, luckily after losing his alias.

The real Bedford-Jones is an elderly man, whose gray hair and precise attire give him rather the appearance of a retired foreign diplomat. His hobby is stamp collecting, and his collection of Japan is said to be one of the finest in existence. At present writing he is en route to Morocco, and when this appears in print he will probably be somewhere on the Mojave Desert in company with Erle Stanley Gardner.

Questioned as to the main facts in his life, he declared there was only one main fact, but it was not for publication; that his life had been uneventful except for numerous financial losses, and that his only adventures lay in evading adventurers. In his younger years he was something of an athlete, but the encroachments of age preclude any active pursuits except that of motoring. He is usually to be found poring over his stamps, working at his typewriter, or laboring in his California rose garden, which is one of the sights of Cathedral Cañon, near Palm Springs.

www.ingramcontent.com/pod-product-compliance
Lightning Source LLC
Chambersburg PA
CBHW050128030726
47505CB00007B/2087